DARK IS THE GRAVE

A DCI BONE SCOTTISH CRIME THRILLER

(BOOK 1)

T G REID

GLASS WORK PRESS

COPYRIGHT

DARK IS THE GRAVE

GLASS WORK PRESS

DEDICATION

To Barry, Gordon, Jon, and Dave… You made me do it.

PROLOGUE

Darkness. Pit-black, impenetrable nothing. PC Hazel Garvey squeezes her eyelids tight and reopens. Still total blackout. She blinks again and again, hoping for some kind of adjustment or definition to emerge. She tries to call out, but there's something rammed inside her mouth, blocking the escape route for her scream. Instinctively, she reaches to grab at the obstruction, but her hands are locked, restrained somewhere behind and beneath her. She is prostrate, her legs folded in, and knees pushed up against an invisible object. She twists her body to try to free her wrists, but the bonds tighten, forcing her clenched fists to bury deeper into the base of her spine. Panic. Her breathing accelerates. Panting. Hyperventilation.

NO!

She diverts her brain to focus on her training, eight years of police experience and hard-earned frontline graft. She inhales deeply to slow her galloping heart. *Try to remember. What? Who?* The sludge engulfing her mind slides, and scenes slither past in haphazard and tangled succession. The frantic, noisy bar. The Fells Inn. Their usual haunt. Her team crowded around a table congested with empty glasses and cigarette packets. Everyone drinking, laughing, taking the piss, the usual banter. A birthday celebration for Fiona.

The movie reel judders. *What next? Fucking remember!* Fiona on her feet, face flushed, happy. A toast. Howls of laughter. *I fell off my chair. Was I pissed?* In the loo, retching in the sink. *I left early.* She racks her brain. Two drinks and then taxi rank. *Why was I pissed on only two drinks — why?* She remembers the nausea and fleeing before she spewed again. She would never live it down. *What next?* Nothing. The jittering reel freeze-frames, and the screen blackens once more. *Only two drinks?* And then it hits her. She'd been spiked. *Fuck!* Somewhere in the bar, somebody loaded her vodka. *But who?*

She holds her breath and listens. Silence. She twists her neck. Her cheek brushes against something rough. A blanket — or a sack? A loud clack above her head, like a door opening — a pinhole of light appears, a tiny fissure in a deep pothole. She jerks back, trying to see. But something grabs her arms and legs. She hears the wind and the rustle of trees, and in the distance, a solitary crow crying out. And now the crunch of footsteps on gravel, her body bobbing up and down. Someone is carrying her. She kicks out and lunges sideways. But the grip is too tight, and the footsteps remain steady and assured. Five, six, seven, eight steps, she counts to remember details that might be useful later, when she escapes and apprehends whoever is doing this to her. The footsteps stop.

Breathing. Not just hers. A man. She moans — trying to formulate the word 'Police'. But something suddenly yanks at her hair, wrenching off whatever was covering her eyes, then the grip around her legs releases, and she rolls sideways, tumbling over and over and crash-landing onto a granite-hard bed of rocks and rubble. The impact smashes her cheekbone and pops her shoulder from its socket. Electrostatic, white-hot pain shoots across her chest and roars in her skull. She screams, but her agony remains stifled by the gag.

She peels open her eyes, but only one complies. Dazzling daylight explodes in her retina. Twisting her head, she forces the lid to open and adjust to the blinding glare. Training, she repeats. Ignores the pain. She twists again. To her left a high wall of — what? She squints again — mud and dirt. She turns back to the light. A silhouette emerges, as though from the heart of the sun. A towering figure. A beast. Looming over her like Frankenstein's abomination. An object glistens in the sun's rays. A gun or a knife? The beast's arm shifts left and right. Now she can see. It is her police ID. She moans again and kicks out, but the pain in her shoulder forces her to stop.

The monster disappears. She scans her surroundings again. Wet clay surrounds her, eight to ten feet high. She shifts her weight from her shoulder and slides her body towards the side wall. The rumble of an engine makes her stop. *A tractor or — No!* The muddy pit she has been dropped into is a grave. Her grave.

A tyre appears at the edge of the precipice, and a digger's boom teeters overhead. With the deafening screech of hydraulic fluid racing through gears, its laden bucket spills a quarter of a ton of excavated mud and rocks onto PC Garvey's legs.

'NO!' Her muffled plea is futile.

The tyres retreat, then moments later return. A second load spews from the loader, and a third, burying her chest and compressing her rib cage until it cracks. And as the fatal fourth tsunami of sodden clay and rubble pummels her skull into the muddy ground, PC Garvey sends one final desperate prayer as the last of her shortened life is crushed out of her lungs.

ONE

D CI Duncan Bone turned over onto his back, his breathing shallow and his eyes flickering rapidly under the lids. He was dreaming. The same dream as last night, and the night before that. Over and over, and always the same, like some demented movie stuck on reruns. The dead of night, raining hard, Bone running at full pelt down a deserted street, feet slapping across saturated ground. Rushing into a soot-blackened tenement building, leaping over debris and human detritus spewed across the near-derelict floor, taking the stairs three at a time — the thick, suffocating darkness devouring him as he climbed. Reaching the top floor, he lunged towards door number six, the digit hanging precariously from the frame and swinging wildly from side to side. He kicked at the paint-blistered surface with full force. The door rattled, but the lock held fast. Bone kicked again and again, but still the door refused to give. He stopped. The handle juddered, and then slowly it turned.

He cried out, "NO!"

His skull filled with an ear-piercing scream, and in an explosion of eye-socket-searing heat and light, the door was obliterated, and a white-hot fireball engulfed Bone's body in a flesh-incinerating blast of unbearable pain.

Bone woke in panic, grasping at his throat. His heart was racing, his head spinning like an out-of-control 747 spiralling towards the ground. He fumbled at his bedside cabinet for the glass of water he had filled the night before, choking down two, three, four gulps. His airway cleared, and oxygen flooded his lungs, his heart rate falling as he inhaled deeply. After a few moments, the electrostatic hiss of the retreating nightmare faded, and he let out a long sigh of exhausted anxiety. He stretched his arm across the bed, searching for the familiar reassuring warmth of Alice's sleeping body. And then his boy, Michael, would run in, climb onto the bed, and jump on his chest until he tickled the giggling toddler into submission… But then, as ever, the stark reality hit home. They were gone, banished by the PTSD that had driven a battering ram through his marriage, through his family. Now, tickling his son had to be DBS checked and timetabled by solicitors and courts, by the police counselling service, and by his ex-wife, who saved her smiles for her future man, who would come as soon as night turned into day.

He sat up and peered into the gloom squeezing through his curtains. His alarm clock read 5:30 a.m.; time had stopped three years ago when his world ended in a bang.

In the bathroom, Bone splashed water on his face and patted gently at the pinkish scar running from his temple, down the length of his drawn, pallid cheek and disappearing into a thick beard that smothered his once-chiselled Hollywood features. When the explosion had ripped through the suspect's flat, it had blown Bone through the wall and out into the landing and the suspect into a thousand pieces. After he'd endured a two-week coma and numerous emergency operations, the surgeon had told Bone it was beyond good fortune that he was still alive, and that if the tiny shard of shrapnel had impacted his skull any lower, he would have been pushing up the weeds.

Bone pulled at the skin below his left eye. The bullet-punch had turned the iris from pale blue to a near-burgundy red, giving him the appearance of a down-on-his luck Terminator, as his smart-arse neighbour had told him when he'd finally been discharged from hospital. The fragment of the killer's femur was still lodged in there, adjacent to the brain stem, too deep and too dangerous to dig out. The surgeon said it was partly responsible for the savage intensity of the initial PTSD that ran him off the road and over a cliff edge, pushing him to the brink of suicide. But now, nearly a year on, despite the occasional hallucinations and odd momentary panic attacks, his terrors and shakes had sufficiently diminished to allow some kind of existence in the world. Returning to work was another matter altogether, but for now, uneventful trips to the supermarket and a beer once in a while at his local was good enough for him. He pressed his finger against the entry wound scar and rubbed at it gently, a comfort habit he'd developed during his convalescence. He sighed again, flicked the bathroom light off, and retreated downstairs in search of coffee.

On his way past the front door, he checked for mail. A padded envelope dangled from the letterbox. He yanked it through and carried on to the kitchen. Dirty dishes piled up on the worktop and in the sink, the kitchen table strewn with old newspapers and junk mail. Housework had never been his strong point, and now, alone in his pokey two-bed flat, it all seemed rather pointless. He filled the kettle and, searching empty cupboards for a mug, dug one out from under a teetering shanty town of unwashed crockery. Rinsing out the mouldy tide mark around the rim, he poured himself a strong black Colombian — about the only thing in the flat worth cherishing. Dropping the envelope on top of the mountain of chaos on the table, he slumped down on a chair by the window and guzzled his coffee.

He glanced over at the calendar dangling from a hook on the kitchen door: 5th October, counselling day. *Bugger.* He contemplated calling in sick. He couldn't face it today. Outside, it was blowing a hooley, and the rain battered against the rusty crittall window, rattling it in its frame, reminding him of his recurring nightmare.

Jesus. That nails it.

He took another sip and closed his eyes. Then his son ran into the kitchen and climbed up on his knee.

"Can I have a sip?"

"No," Bone said, shaking his head.

"Coco Pops!" Michael shouted.

Bone opened his eyes, and the memory dissolved. He checked the time—7:03. Jumping up, he returned to the bedroom to get dressed and make a run for it. If he was quick, he would make it to Alice's house before they set off for school.

Bone arrived, out of breath and soaked through. He'd run most of the way, avoiding the town centre and the gauntlet of small-town nosiness, but now wished he'd given in to his laziness and taken the car. In his hurry to leave, he'd forgotten to put on his coat, and his shirt was clinging to him like an undersized diver's wet suit. He raced up Alice's small front garden, almost tumbling over his son's trike lying across the path. He rang the buzzer. No reply. He rang again.

The speaker clicked, and a tiny voice squeaked, "Hello?"

"Michael, it's Dad. Could you let me in, son?"

After more clicking and fumbling, another voice came on.

"Duncan, is that you?" Alice said briskly.

"Yes, can you let me in? It's pissing down out here."

"We're on our way out. I'm taking Michael to school."

"I know. I thought maybe I could take him this morning?"

The buzzer whistled and went dead.

"Alice? Alice!" He pressed the button again.

The front door swung open, and Alice appeared, flushed and harassed, holding Michael with one hand while balancing an armful of his school paraphernalia in the other. Michael disengaged himself from her tight grip and ran out to meet his dad as Alice's hair fell out of its band, the long curls tumbling over her face.

"Jesus," she groaned, grabbing at it.

"Dad!" Michael said, jumping up into Bone's wide, welcoming arms.

"Whoa! You've got bigger," Bone said with a wide smile. "And heavier."

Alice clicked the front door shut. "Come on, Michael, we're going to be late."

"I want Dad to take me. Can't he, please?" Michael pleaded, his round, freckled, six-year-old face folding into an irresistible pout.

"Come on," Alice insisted, her tone and resistance hardening.

"It's no bother," Bone interjected. "I'd be happy to."

Alice turned on him. "We've talked about this, Duncan. We agreed to access times. *You* agreed."

"I know, but I miss this naughty wee face," he said, pinching Michael's cheek.

"No. This isn't on," Alice pushed back. "Put him down. Come on, Michael. We need to go."

"Just one walk to school, that's all," Bone persisted. "It's only twenty minutes, and then I'll abide by the rules, I promise."

Alice looked at Bone, her eyes clouding over as though recognising the pain racked across his features, connecting for just a flicker of a moment. Then she puffed out her cheeks. "Okay, this is a one-off, all right?" she said.

"Woohoo!" Michael let out an excited yell and pummelled Bone's chest with his fists.

"Thank you," Bone said, smiling. "You have no idea."

"Oh, I do, but I mean it. We stick to what was agreed in future, okay?"

Bone nodded, but he was already distracted with tickling his boy, who was giggling fit to burst.

Alice shook her head. "You'll need these?" She thrust Michael's schoolbag, lunchbox, and raincoat towards him.

Bone set the boy down and took the items, his hand brushing against Alice's. She pulled away.

"Go! You're going to be late," she said.

"So, walking or camel ride?" Bone asked his son, who was holding on to Bone's hand as tightly as any six-year-old could.

"Camel!" Michael squealed, beaming.

"All aboard then." Bone picked up Michael again, propping him up on top of his shoulders. "And off we go!"

The boy jiggled about in excitement.

"Could all passengers refrain from sudden movements, as the camel's a grumpy lump?" Bone boomed like a platform announcer.

Michael laughed and sat up straight, riding high on being with his dad. When they reached the school gate, Bone set Michael down and handed him his stuff. One of the teachers, Miss Champling, an elderly, stern-faced woman, hurried children inside with brisk flicks of the wrist. *Oh God, not her.* She spotted the Bone and his son loitering at the gate and approached. Bone pretended not to see her.

"Michael Bone, come along. You don't want to keep your teacher waiting, now do you?" She shot Bone a withering look.

"I'm just saying goodbye," Bone said. He kissed the boy on the forehead. "You be a good boy, okay? Do what Mum says."

He crossed his eyes playfully, and Michael laughed.

"I'll see you in a wee while."

"Hurry up, Michael," the teacher cut in again.

"Just give me a minute." Bone's anger rose.

"There is an important assembly this morning, Mr—?"

"Bone."

"Mr Bone, Michael's father?"

No, Mr Bone the local paedo, come to abduct another kid, Bone thought. "Yes, his father," he muttered.

"Well, I must say it is very good to finally meet you," she said, with a strong whiff of sarcasm.

"Likewise, Miss Champling," Bone fired back. "I've heard so much about you."

"All good, I hope," she said, a crooked smile escaping from her thin-lipped mouth.

"Bye, Dad," Michael said and, grappling with his bags, he pushed past the teacher and disappeared into the school.

"So, are we likely to be seeing more of you?" Miss Champling asked Bone.

"Well, I'd certainly like to see more of Michael at least," Bone snapped, and left Miss Champling to ponder his barbed response.

Back at his flat, Bone felt buoyed by the morning's turn of events. Perhaps there was a flicker of light to be found in his relationship with Alice. He had trained his brain not to hope too much, but for the first time since the explosion and his injury, the particles of possibility bounced around in his chest, a near-forgotten sensation he thought he'd never experience again.

Glancing round the carnage in the kitchen, he decided to capitalise on his mood and give the flat a long overdue deep clean. Starting with the table, he scooped up all the old newspapers and junk flyers and dumped them in the bin. But then he spotted the envelope from the morning's mail. The address was typed, using his full title, Detective Chief Inspector Duncan Bone, Esq. *Esquire? Who writes Esquire these days unless it's a joke?* Grabbing a pair of scissors, he sliced across the seal. Inside was a card. He cleared a space on the table and laid the card down. On the front was a photograph of a skeleton waving from a coffin, with the phrase *Just checking you're not dead yet,* written underneath in a black Gothic font, like something a funeral parlour would use. He opened it out, and on one side was a typed message:

TO LAZY BONER

A WEE WORD

FROM THE ARSEHOOZ

Bone smiled. It was from his colleagues at the Rural Crime Unit, or the Arsehooz, as the team had affectionately christened themselves. Since his injury and subsequent sick leave, he'd had very little contact. He'd been too ill to face them, and when Scotland's police commissioner got in touch, to let him know he'd been awarded a medal of honour for his bravery, he'd politely turned it down. He'd inadvertently obliterated the prime suspect — hardly honourable or worth celebrating, he'd concluded. Since then, he'd only seen one member of the team — DI Walker, his second-in-command — when he bumped into her in the queue in Scotsave. She'd looked pleased to see him, but he wasn't in the best of places that day and had given her short shrift. And that was it, so while the card was a rather unexpected surprise, it was odd as it seemed a little out of the blue. Maybe something funny had happened and they wanted to share, or maybe they thought it was time to start taking the piss out of their boss again. Whatever it was, Bone's day was turning out to be a little better than how it had started.

He flipped the card over, expecting a few scribbled expletives and choice not-so-goodwill messages. But the card was blank. He cautiously peered inside the envelope in case there was something rude still lingering in there. A tiny black object had caught in the bottom corner. He shook the envelope, and the object flew out and landed on the carpet a few feet away. He picked it up. It was a micro USB stick.

"Oh Jesus," he muttered. "What offensive horrors have they sent me?" He winced at the thought but felt quietly pleased they were thinking about him, even if only to take the piss. Pulling himself out of his chair, he fetched his laptop from the bedroom and set it on the table, opened the lid, and switched it on. Nothing.

"Bollocks." He went back to the bedroom, and after a few minutes of searching and swearing, he returned with the mains cable.

He tried again. This time the laptop kicked into life, and he impatiently entered his password. He examined the USB, trying to work out which end or way round to stick the thing into the machine. He tried one way, then another, until finally it slotted into a port and the USB identified itself on the screen. He clicked on the icon, and a single, untitled video file popped up. He hovered the mouse over the icon for a second and then clicked again. His ancient laptop took a few moments to register his request, then the screen went black, flickered, and a wall of fuzzy lines appeared.

"Fuck," he said, fumbling again with the USB.

The screen dissolved to black, and then a scratchy, washed-out moving image appeared. Bone shifted the laptop away from the light to try and improve the resolution. There was a figure lying in some kind of hole or trench. The hiss intensified. The figure moved or writhed around. He peered closer. It was a woman. She had what appeared to be black packing tape wrapped around her head, with a section removed, exposing one eye.

Bone jerked backwards, the familiarity of the images assaulting his senses. From nowhere, dirt and rocks tumbled onto the flailing body. Grotesque scenes from his past thundered through his mind like a raging tsunami of horror. The 'snuff' mp4s that had landed week after week in his email, recording the slow, agonising deaths of three police officers, buried, cremated, and the last — before the monster had finally been cornered — a young constable slowly being drained of blood and embalmed, while still alive.

Not again!

Bone thumped the keyboard, trying to make the video stop. Through the hiss came the sound of a digger's engine growing louder and louder. In desperation, he grabbed the mains cable and yanked it from the machine. The video disappeared, and the screen returned to black. Bone collapsed onto the floor, the panic galloping out of control in his chest. He grabbed at the floor, the room spinning. Stumbling to his feet, he retreated to the bedroom, fleeing the possibility that the video could start playing again of its own free will.

After an hour of going over and over what kind of deviant bastard would send a carbon copy video reconstruction — if that's what it was — the initial shock and fear of the after-effects of his injuries he'd worked hard to come to terms with gave way to anger, and then to rage. Just when he thought he might be turning a corner, this shit happened. It was always the way. It was as though he were being punished for fucking everything up. But this was punishment of seismic proportions — or the sickest prank ever played.

"Fuck this!" he growled.

He searched his pocket for his mobile and, scrolling through his contacts, stopped at Detective Superintendent Gallacher's number. His finger hovered over the call button. He knew he'd have to report it; something as deranged as this could not be ignored. But maybe he should call another squad anonymously? Reopening old wounds could set him back again. He winced. How much farther back could he go? His fury superseded any fear of a relapse. As far as he was concerned, a relapse might be the least of his worries. He pressed the call button, and the number rang.

TWO

"Now there's a sight for very sore eyes." Detective Superintendent Roy Gallacher stood in Bone's doorway, his imposing bulk blocking most of the light from the close. "I'm loving the *Nanook of the North* look," he said, nodding at the forest of hair almost entirely consuming Bone's face and head. "Christ, if I'd known, I'd have brought some fucking loose change with me."

His sweary athleticism with the English language was legendary in the force. As a kid who'd survived alcoholic parents and a fractured upbringing in and out of care, he'd had to fight for the hardest wins his entire life, making his meteoric rise through the ranks all the a more miraculous achievement.

"Hello to you, too," Bone said, ushering the DSU into his flat.

"What's that god-awful stench?" Gallacher asked as he followed Bone past the kitchen on their way to the living room.

"That would be me, sir," Bone half joked.

"Well, you look like a man in bad need of a job," Gallacher said. "I hope this is what our unexpected reunion's about?"

"Would you like a coffee?" Bone asked, ignoring Gallacher's question.

"Aye, that would be lovely, as long as Rentokil has mucked out the cup first." The DSU squinted round the carnage of neglect surrounding them. "Seriously, though, it *is* good to see you. How the hell have you been?" He frowned at Bone's facial hair again. "Stupid question. Shite, as I can see."

"It's not been easy, that's for sure."

"Well, you suffered quite a trauma, and the Peek-a-boo case. It got to us all. You know I had some one-to-ones as well."

"I didn't know that."

"Oh aye. There's always that risk in our jobs that the evil bastards will get under our skin. I knew all of those PCs and their families. And it was wrecking-ball horrendous." He sighed. "Anyhow, I sorted it. But what I'm saying is, you were never alone with this, but you shut yourself away, and I'm not sure that was a good thing to do."

"So, how are the troops?" Bone changed the subject.

"Oh, you know — the same bunch of arseholes as they ever were, though missing the biggest one, obviously." Gallacher smiled.

"Who's the new DCI?"

"You mean who's holding the fort till you get back? That would be the effervescent DS Mullens."

19

"Oh Jesus. That's risky, isn't it? Giving that big eejit even more power to punch people," Bone joked.

"I know, but nobody wanted to step into your shoes."

"What about Rhona?"

"I asked. Well, I practically begged DI Walker to fill in, but she refused. You're a tough act to follow, and I think she thought it was disrespectful or something."

"Don't get me wrong, Mullens is a fine copper, and the go-to person if you're looking for a tag wrestling partner. But DCI? I bet you've had a few sleepless nights worrying about what he might do to get you all sacked?"

"Luckily it's been all quiet on the Western Front, a couple of domestic assaults, some gangland shenanigans. Would you believe that the Northfield crew have switched from class A to cattle rustling? Can you imagine the field day Mullens had with that?"

Bone smirked.

"So you still haven't told me why you've invited me over to your slurry tank of a flat."

Bone retrieved the laptop from the kitchen and, setting it up on the living room table, he booted it up. "This morning, I received this in the post."

He hit the play button on the file. The screen hissed again, and the scene of horror returned. While Gallacher watched, Bone retreated to the kitchen. From there, he could still hear the rumble of the digger cutting through the static. He opened the window and focused on the sound of the rain pelting off the roof of an old tin shed in one of the gardens below. After a few minutes, Gallacher appeared in the doorway, his face ashen.

"What the fuck is that?"

"My words exactly, sir."

"When did you say you got this?"

"This morning."

"Is it some kind of sick joke?"

"Yup, I said that, too," Bone replied.

"I mean — it's identical."

"I know."

"It's got to be a prank. Somebody's set this up, surely?"

"You would hope so."

"But that's just fucking evil. There's nothing funny about it."

"Aye, here's the card." Bone picked it up from the table.

"Put it down!" Gallacher urged.

Bone complied.

"We'll need to get the SOC team onto this. I don't have a good feeling."

"I thought the card was from you guys. It says from the arsehooz."

"Clearly, no. I don't think even Mullens would sink that low for a laugh. But it's someone who knows the nickname."

Bone nodded.

"What's the postmark on the envelope?" Gallacher asked.

"Glasgow, but that's the central sorting office, so that doesn't really tell us much," Bone replied.

"Jesus Christ. This is all you need." Gallacher shook his head.

"I'm okay."

"Are you sure?"

"I'm more angry than anything, to be honest."

"It's shocking. Why would they send it to you?"

"Some wee sicko with a grudge, maybe? I've banged up quite a few heid-the-baws over the years."

"Listen," Gallacher interrupted. "Let me take this. I'll get forensics onto it and see what we can do."

Bone nodded.

"Have you got something I can take it in, so that we don't contaminate it any further?" Gallacher looked around the cluttered floor. "Difficult I know." He raised an eyebrow.

"A carrier bag is the best I can do," Bone said, snatching up one from a chair.

"It'll have to do." Gallacher fished a disposable glove out of his pocket and pulled it on before dropping the USB into the carrier bag. "I'll need that card and envelope, too."

At the door, Gallacher stopped. "I'll ring you as soon as I hear anything, okay? Hopefully it's just some attention-seeking nutjob and the team will sort him out."

Bone nodded.

"And not to worry, but keep your door locked."

"Oh, I can still look after myself, sir."

"That's good to hear." Gallacher held out his hand. "Well, despite the unpleasant surprise, it's good to see you, Duncan." He smiled.

"Likewise," Bone replied.

And with a brief wave, the DSU was gone.

The next morning, Bone's mobile sparked up. Falling out of bed, he rifled through the piles of clothes on the floor until he finally located it. Still blurry-eyed from sleep, he fumbled with the buttons and finally found the answer button.

"Hello?" Bone croaked.

Silence.

"Hello? Who is this?"

The line clicked and went dead.

"Hello! Is there anyone there?"

It rang again, and Bone almost dropped it. "Fuck sake."

He hit the button again.

'Who is this?'

"Detective Superintendent Gallacher, your boss?" Gallacher's broad Govan accent growled through the speaker.

"Sorry, sir. I've just woken up, and my phone has been going mental."

"I'm ringing..." Gallacher paused. "It's the recording — I need to talk to you. It might be best if you come in."

"In?"

"To the station."

"When?"

"Now, if you can."

Bone hesitated.

"Are you there?" Gallacher asked.

"I'm not sure, sir. It's been a while."

"You can come in through the back if you prefer. We can keep it low profile. I just think it would be better to speak face to face."

Bone pressed his finger into the puncture mark on his temple.

"As a matter of urgency." Gallacher was insistent.

"I'll come but I don't want any fuss from the team, okay?"

"Guaranteed."

THREE

DCI Bone's ancient, bottle-green Saab 96 approached the brutalist 70s concrete monstrosity of Kilwinnoch Police Station. For a smallish rural town, its nick was unusually large, perhaps to accommodate the then newly formed Rural Crime Unit. Or in a heady moment of indulgent glamour, the regional council anticipated some optimistic surge in criminal activity. But while the town had its fair share of headbangers and the odd major incident, the building always felt rather barren and empty. Bone hadn't clapped eyes on its ugly fizzog since his injury, but there were no pangs of nostalgia for the place.

He parked up opposite, adding another layer of detail to the street's 70s time warp, and started towards the entrance. A couple of uniforms emerged from the front door and descended the stairs. Bone turned his back to avoid being recognised. When the coast was clear, he headed round the side to the back entrance but then changed his mind.

Bugger it! Enough was enough. It was time to face the demons. He ascended the stairs and went in.

A burly faced desk sergeant glanced up. "Can I help you?"

"Sergeant Brody. How are you?"

The sergeant stared at Bone's hairy features for a moment, and then a smile of recognition broadened across his portly face. "DCI Bone?"

"How's it going?" Bone smiled.

"Sorry, sir, I didn't recognise you with the er — forestation."

"You're looking leaner since I saw you last." Bone hoped he sounded sincere.

"You think? My wife's got me on that cabbage diet. I'm losing weight, but my family have abandoned the house through fear of being gassed to death, or an explosion." His face suddenly contorted as though he'd sucked on some nettles. "Sorry, I didn't mean to—" he stuttered.

Bone tutted away his faux pas.

"So, how you doing now? I hear you've been through it," Brody continued, the hole he was diggingwidening with every word.

"Is the DSU in?" Bone changed the subject.

"Oh — er...aye, sir. I'll buzz you through, unless you have your ID. It'll still work, I'm sure," the sergeant said.

"Just let me in, that'll be great."

"No bother."

Brody buzzed the access door to the offices, and Bone cautiously entered.

He took the stairs to the third floor. A door opened at the end of the corridor, and DC Will Harper's bespectacled baby face peeked round.

Shit.

"Excuse me!" Harper called after Bone and stepped out into the corridor. "This is a secure area."

Idiot. Where does he think we are, the Pentagon?

"What are you doing in here?" Harper continued, his voice elevating a couple of octaves.

Resolving to have a bit of fun, Bone veered straight towards the increasingly startled young detective.

"You need to go back downstairs, and the desk sergeant will attend to you," Harper said.

Bone quickened his pace, and Harper retreated.

"Stop!" he cried in a soprano screech, fit for an opening night at La Scala.

"Boo!" Bone roared, throwing up his hands.

Harper's expression migrated from pant-soiling terror to confusion and finally settled on recognition and relief.

"Jesus Christ, sir. I was just about to drop you to the floor there," Harper puffed, his cheeks glowing like a freshly spanked arse.

"Oh aye, I bet."

"I take it you've heard then?" Harper said, attempting to get his shit together.

"No, what?"

A door at the end of the corridor opened, and Gallacher stepped out.

"What's all the bloody commotion?" He spotted Bone. "Come inside."

Bone obliged with Harper in tow.

"Not you," the DSU said.

Harper reluctantly retreated back down the corridor.

Bone scanned the room as he entered. Everything was pretty much as he remembered it, though even more obsessively tidy, if that were possible. Two of Bone's colleagues stood by the window. DS Mark Mullens, a six-foot-four, ginger-topped fridge-freezer on legs; was flanked by DI Rhona Walker. Flushed as always, and even in her sharp regulation suit, she still looked like she'd just blown in off the last ferry from Lewis.

"I thought we were keeping this low-key," Bone complained.

"There have been some developments." Gallacher grimaced.

Bone looked back at the two detectives. A half-smile fleeted across Mullens' face, and Walker nodded a professional hello. After nearly a year, that was quite an underwhelming welcome back. Something was seriously wrong.

"Take a seat," Gallacher continued, sitting at his well-ordered desk.

"I'd prefer to stand if that's okay. I won't be staying long," Bone said, feeling ambushed.

"Sit your arse down," the DSU insisted.

Bone reluctantly obliged.

"We've been looking into the video you were sent," Gallacher said, looking Bone right in the eye.

"And?" Bone asked impatiently.

"We've received information to indicate that the horror show is not some kind of re-enactment or hoax."

"What — it's real? The woman?" Bone's heart pounded.

"Last week, our colleagues in missing persons were investigating the disappearance of a woman called Hazel Garvey," Gallacher continued.

"And?" Bone asked, but already knew where this was heading.

"This morning, a police officer from Campsie Fells station confirmed that the woman in the video was indeed Hazel Garvey, PC Hazel Garvey."

"Shit — a copper?"

"A very *good* copper, a twice-decorated copper."

"Jesus Christ, not again." Bone closed his eyes.

"I'm afraid there's more."

"Go on," Bone replied, sighing.

"PC Garvey is the wife of Ross McLean."

"Not McLean the lawyer?"

"Chief Officer to be more precise."

"Wasn't he that knobhead working on the Peek-a-boo case for the procurator fiscal?" Mullens piped up.

"Yup," Bone replied. "And now it would seem, promoted to head honcho, just to add to the fun.

"So are we looking at some kind of vendetta?" DI Walker jumped in.

"These are questions that we need to ask," Gallacher said. "But at this stage, as we have not yet recovered a body, we have to throw everything we can into finding PC Garvey. If this *is* a copycat, then we know that Peek-a-boo kept his victims alive for three or four days."

"But the video… No one could possibly survive that?" Walker added.

"We can't make any presumptions. Eyes, ears, minds, and instinct open."

"Evil fuckturd," Mullens snarled.

"Thank you, Detective." Gallacher scowled and stepped back, shaking his head.

Bone clenched his fists. "But why did this cockroach send the tape to me and not McLean, as Peek-a-boo did with the families of his victims?"

"Whoever has done this has intimate knowledge of the case," Gallacher replied. "The video bears an uncannily accurate resemblance to the original Peek-a-boo tapes, and clearly the perpetrator has targeted you for a reason."

"So it has to be a vendetta then?" Bone glanced over at Walker.

"That's why I called you in."

Bone froze for a moment to process what his boss was saying. "Hold on — surely you're not expecting me back?"

"I'm not expecting, I'm ordering, DCI Bone." Gallacher's strained smile tightened further.

Bone leapt from his chair. "Could I have a private word?"

The DSU followed Bone out of the office.

At the end of the corridor, Gallacher took a left through a fire door which led out onto the roof. If anything, the wind had picked up strength, and rain was still in the air. Striding over to the stairs, he turned and held up his hand.

"Before you say anything, hear me out, Duncan," Gallacher said, his carefully lacquered hair making a valiant attempt to flee the top of his balding pate. "This morning, I had the procurator fiscal's office on the phone, followed shortly after by an interesting chat with my old police training college mate, Peter Laverty."

"The chief constable?"

"The big guns. It would appear McLean's throwing his influential weight around and blaming the RCU for fucking up the Peek-a-boo case."

"Me, you mean."

"No, Duncan, me." The DSU winced. "I'm trying to head off a full-force shitstorm here. They want McLean's partner found and the perpetrator caught before this escalates further."

"Well, obviously."

"As a favour, Laverty has blocked the investigation being handed over to another unit, for now, but we are rammed up against it here." A gust of wind almost blew them both over the edge. "I need you back here leading your team."

"My team? I don't think so," Bone replied.

"They trust you and no one else."

"They are the finest crime unit in Scotland. They don't need me."

"Duncan," Gallacher shifted tactics and took a first name approach. "This is a copycat of the case you led.

You have detailed and microscopic knowledge of the crime and the killer. And as you said, the tape was sent to you for a reason."

"But McLean thinks I messed up. Won't my return just give Edinburgh the reason they need to hang us up by the gonads?"

"McLean is angry, and Laverty is no numpty. He has enough professional nous to know that this is our case and you are the best DCI to lead it."

Bone shook his head. "I don't need this. I'm trying to get back with Alice and see my kid more. A *lot* more. I can't jeopardise that."

"I've spoken to your rehab team," Gallacher cut in. "They've told me you're ready to return."

"Oh, thanks," Bone snapped back. "My so-called rehab is my business. What goes on there is confidential."

"As your commanding officer, I have a duty to protect my squad. I have every right to make enquiries. They said nothing other than that you were fit for service, but the decision was entirely yours."

"My decision, exactly," Bone snarled. "So don't start throwing orders at me. I'm still on sick leave, in case you haven't noticed."

"Duncan, please. I'm desperate here." Gallacher leaned in, sheltering them both from the gale. "Look we've known each other a long time. I know you. You are ready, and you know you are ready. You can't bury yourself away in that hovel of yours forever. Come on, don't you think you owe it to PC Garvey and your team?"

"Oh, the guilt card. I wondered how long it would be before that surfaced," Bone snapped. "I'm an Olympic medal winner when it comes to that particular emotion." Despite his protestations, he knew his boss was not going to let this go and events were conspiring against him to refuse his boss's order. He winced. His heart was roaring at him to take the emergency stairs, but his head was conducting a military-style coup d'état. There were just too many tangled threads twisting around his life again that needed to be tied off, once and for all.

"So what's it to be?" Gallacher persisted. "I need a decision, right now. Come back in or take the fire escape?"

"If I say yes…" Bone started.

"Hallelujah!" Gallacher jumped in.

"*If* I say yes, I'm not going to sit on my arse behind a desk. I lead this case from the ground up, and you let us get on with it — with no interference or politics from the skid marks in Edinburgh."

"I wouldn't have it any other way," Gallacher said, smiling. "In fact, I'll be your human shield."

Bone paused. "Okay," he said finally, the words airborne before he could retract them.

"Welcome back, DCI Bone." Gallacher nodded his approval.

"Let's just take things as they come, okay?" Bone replied.

"Of course."

"Just one thing, though," Bone said as they walked back.

"I'm all ears."

"Can I start tomorrow? There's a couple of things I need to do."

"Seven a.m. sharp."

"Yes, sir."

"Sir? Now that sounds more like it." Gallacher grinned.

"A moment of weakness. It won't happen again."

At the door, Gallacher stopped. "Thank you, Duncan. I owe you," he said with sincerity.

"I might hold you to that," Bone replied, and they went back in.

FOUR

By the time Bone got back to the sinkhole he called home, he'd resigned himself to thinking he'd made the right decision. It was time. Time to move forward and drag his self-pitying arse out of the quagmire. If he was going to make anything of his life with Alice and his son, he needed to put the wheels back on and steer himself towards the light instead of wallowing, lost and alone, in the darkness of a past that had ransacked his world.

In the bathroom, he rummaged around the cabinet in search of his shaving brush, lathered up his beard, and slowly snowploughed his face until his near-forgotten features emerged. He appeared older and leaner, not quite the Hollywood looks he used to feel a little embarrassed to possess, and he liked what he saw. It felt good to remove the mask and shed the weight, and for the first time in months he felt alive and ready to take on whatever lorry load of slurry was coming his way.

In the hall, he pushed at the door of the box room, a place he'd avoided since the accident. The door was stiff, and putting his shoulder to it, he edged it open.

The room was rammed full of boxes and files. Some of the clutter was personal effects recovered from the death scene of his marriage, but stacked up at the back were piles of ring binders and lever arch files. His homework, as he used to call it. Clambering over the chaos, he stretched over a tea chest and grabbed a couple of files from the top of a teetering tower. He opened the first. Some papers spilled out and disappeared between the boxes.

Bugger. Flicking through what was left in the binder, he quickly realised this was not what he was looking for. He checked the second, but the contents related to a domestic murder four years previously. He stretched out again, plucked a large lever arch file from the second mini skyscraper, and opened it up. The first page was labelled, 'Robert Meiklejohn', with 'The Peek-a-boo case,' handwritten underneath in bold red lettering. The words screamed up at him, and his hands shook.

"Here we go," he muttered.

He climbed back out, returned to the living room and dropped the file onto a side table by the window. He pulled up a chair, opened the file, and flicked to the first page. Three faces stared back at him. Victims he'd spent months trying to obliterate from his mind. He pressed his forefinger against the entry wound scar on his temple and proceeded.

PC Katie Edwards, 28, from Lennoxfield station. She was beautiful, elegant, the light of life twinkling in her youthful eyes — until she was buried alive.

The second, PC Maggie Cowley, 37, Strathglennan squad. Peek-a-boo cremated her, filmed it, and sent the recording to her partner.

And the third, the most chilling, PC Gordon Tyrrell, 23, fresh out of police training, only three months into his job at Kilwinnoch nick. Meiklejohn drained his blood — just enough to keep him alive — then pumped four gallons of embalming fluid into the femoral artery in his thigh.

Tyrell's police ID mugshot scowled at Bone as though reprimanding him for not bringing the bastard to justice. Bone sighed. This refresher tour of a serial killer's career was going to be a journey of pain, no doubt about it. He needed a coffee. He closed the file and retreated to the kitchen to gather his mental armies and prepare for a return to battle.

***

Bone woke with a start, gasping for breath, his fists wrapped around sodden sheets. He turned to reach for water, but a figure loomed over him. He tried to pull back or sit up, but his body was paralysed with fear or half-conscious sleep. The figure shifted sideways. Untangling his arm from the sheet, Bone reached out and snatched at the bedside lamp. The figure pushed towards him. He fumbled for the switch but knocked the lamp off the table. As it hit the floor, the bulb exploded. The flash of light momentarily revealed the figure's hideous features: a burnt, disfigured skull of melted skin, exposed bone, and broiled, puckered flesh.

In terror, Bone lashed out, but his flailing fists seemed to pass through the shadow that was now pressing down on him. Bone lunged at the creature but he tumbled out of bed and landed on the floor with a painful thud. Scrambling to his feet, he snatched at the wall until his hand connected with the main light. Frantically, he flicked at the switch and squinted through the glare for the assailant. But the room was deserted. Bar the pounding of his heart in his eardrums, everything was still.

Hallucination. Fuck. He hadn't experienced any for nearly a month. His alarm suddenly screamed to life.

"Jesus!" he yelped, his chest taking another leap of fright. He rubbed his eyes, slumped back down on the side of the bed, and thumped at the top of the clock radio until it stopped its cacophony. "That's all I need."

FIVE

"Here comes the boner!" DS Mullens was first to greet Bone when he entered the incident room, his hulking frame towering over him, an over inflated Lurch from the Addams Family waiting for the next cadaver to arrive at the mortuary.

The room erupted in a volley of applause.

"Welcome back, sir." Mullens extended his hand. "And about bloody time 'cos Andy at the Fells won't tap us any more drinks until you pay the bar bill."

"Bloody hell, I think you've actually grown," Bone replied, wincing as Mullens crushed the life out of his palm. "Have you had a brain transplant?"

"No, but I hear you're due one," Mullens said.

"I walked right into that. Thanks for stepping up," Bone skewered his crushed hand free.

"Well, all I can say is, thank fuck you're back," Mullens continued. "I really don't know how you put up with this shower of a useless hooz of the arse for so long. Unbearable, so it was."

"What happened to the down-and-out who had hijacked your face?" DI Walker said, smiling as she approached.

Originally from the Isle of Lewis, Rhona Walker had cut her teeth as a uniform and then drug squad detective for the Highland division, her keen detective skills helping to take down one of the UK's top cartels. She always joked that she'd requested the transfer to Kilwinnoch for a quiet life, but in truth she'd wanted to work on a murder squad and, in particular, with Bone. Walker's intuitive, no-nonsense approach to policing had immediately impressed Bone, and he'd persuaded the powers that be to put her name forward for promotion. Within a few weeks she had passed her promotion board interview with flying colours and was now a DI and his second-in-command.

"I set the poor thing free." Bone shook her hand.

"Good to see you back in the saddle, sir," DC Will Harper chirped in, lingering at the side like an overeager puppy.

Harper was the most recent arrival, landing right in the middle of the Peek-a-boo case — a baptism of fire for the poor sod. Harper was a computer science graduate and had been recruited to the RCU via the force's new fast-track scheme, much to the derision of his colleagues. But despite his obvious inexperience on the ground and possessing the unlikeliest of looks for any detective on the force, Harper had an IBM-sized geek brain that could decipher the most unintelligible alien computer-speak and unlock any passcode with a single binary-encrypted thought.

"Aye, and I'll be riding your back till you break," Bone replied.

The team let out a collective guffaw.

DS Sheila Baxter, or —as Mullens called her— the *three piece suite*, due to her penchant for wearing what appeared to be her granny's best tweed from head to foot, stood awkwardly by her desk at the window. Bone spotted her familiar world-weary frown and greeted her with a warm smile. While her rather upholstered taste in fashion was deeply questionable, Baxter's knowledge of criminal law, previous cases, suspects and crimes, was legendary. For some inexplicable reason, Baxter had swapped an earlier, more lucrative career as a criminal lawyer for the horrific delights of hardcore homicide, but Bone and the team were glad she had. She was not only one of the brightest cops on the force, she could throw up an arrest report faster than a fart in a wind tunnel, and so was considered an indispensable member of the unit, especially around audit time.

Bone moved farther into the room, and the detectives gathered round.

"Okay, listen up. We are all deeply saddened by recent events. It is a terrible tragedy for PC Garvey, Chief Officer McLean, and their respective families."

"And we're going to dismember the bastard who did this," Mullens cut in.

"Emotions are running very high, but that is precisely what we are *not* going to do, DS Mullens."

Bone shot the detective a stern look. "I'm back to lead this investigation, and we are going to conduct ourselves with the utmost professionalism. We will investigate this case in a level-headed, rational, and systematic manner that befits the honour of our profession, do you understand?"

"Yes, sir," the team mumbled.

"Do I make myself crystal clear?"

"Yes, sir," the team shouted back.

"Good, and contrary to rumour, I'm not entirely doolally, but I have gained this very odd sixth sense that tells me when someone is fucking me over or disobeying my orders."

A smattering of laughter.

"I'm deadly serious. The last thing we need is for some idiot to lose their shit or do something utterly stupid, DS Mullens."

"Sir!"

"Okay, so now that the riot act has been well and truly read, let's get on with doing what we're supposed to."

"Sir?" DC Harper stepped up. "The Peek-a-boo suspect. You know, the one who…"

"Blew me up, yes?" Bone cut in.

Harper pushed his glasses up the bridge of his nose. "He was…the guy, right?"

"Let's clear the air, shall we?" Bone addressed the team again. "We are dealing with a copycat here, someone who knows the Meiklejohn case and is privy to details that were never released to the press or in the public domain."

"So an insider?" Will asked.

Mullens spun round and glared at his new colleague. "Give the wee laddie a lolly."

"Or Peek-a-boo had a big mouth, or an accomplice, and that's what we're here to find out," Bone added. "Right then. What do we know so far?" His question was met by an ominous silence. "Well?"

"All we have at this stage is that PC Garvey failed to return home after attending a colleague's birthday drinks at The Fells Inn," Mullens stepped in. "Her husband, Mr McLean…"

"Chief Officer Advocate McLean," Bone qualified.

"Aye, well, aforementioned baw heed reported her missing the following morning."

"He waited all night?" Bone asked.

"It would seem so. He called her station, and they logged it at…" Mullens lumbered over to his desk and retrieved his notepad. "Eleven twenty-three a.m."

"Nearly lunchtime?"

"Correct."

Bone rubbed the scar on his temple. "Odd."

He turned to DI Walker, who'd been unusually quiet. "Has forensics come back with anything on the card, yet?"

"Nothing yet, sir," Walker said, her Hebridean lilt still undiminished by her exodus to the mainland.

"DC Harper," Bone said.

The young detective almost jumped out of his oversized suit.

"Can you go down to records and dig out the Peek-a-boo files, including all the recordings? I need you to run a comparison with the new video. I'm sure you have special Jedi powers you can harness on that computer of yours."

"Wow, I'd skip the popcorn if I were you, Will," Mullens joked.

But no one laughed.

"As DC Harper has just illustrated," Bone continued, "we need to eliminate any doubt that this could be the same killer and that Meiklejohn was the wrong man."

"But the evidence was conclusive that he was the evil bastard who killed those officers," Walker cut in.

"We know that, and anyone in their right mind knows that, but we need to have all our ducks in a row, because once the press get a hold of this, it'll be like feeding time at the zoo."

"Pond life," Mullens mumbled.

"And that's why we all need to keep schtum — no blabbing to friends or relatives, not even partners. Clear? They're going to find out soon enough, but we need as much space as we can right now. Has anyone interviewed the husband yet, I mean formally?"

"I think family liaison have been round to his house, but he wasn't answering," Walker said.

"Okay, and what about PC Garvey's movements immediately before, during, and after her pub visit?"

"Uniforms are at the pub now, I believe, but no one from here has been down there yet," Walker added.

"What about pub CCTV, and on her route to the pub?"

Silence.

"And her colleagues at Campsie Fells station?"

Silence again.

"God's sake. Come on, people. It's a good job I'm back." Bone shook his head. "Right, Mullens, get your arse down to The Fells Inn tout de suite and interview the landlord and bar staff. Check any CCTV footage, if they have any, and track down the punters who were there that night."

Mullens checked his watch. "And just in time for their half-price breakfast bap," he said, licking his lips.

Bone turned to DS Baxter, who was rummaging manically in her handbag.

"Sheila," he said.

She looked up.

"Aye?" she replied, then resumed her battle with her bag.

"DS Baxter," Bone repeated.

"Sorry, sir," the detective croaked, "I've lost my lighter."

"Still not jacked them in then?" Bone asked.

"Oh God, I've tried."

"I need you to go through Advocate McLean's prosecution case against Meiklejohn," Bone continued. "But also go back farther and check his record — former prosecutions, wins, losses, and search for anything anomalous."

"All of them?" Baxter asked.

"Yup."

"Sir?" Baxter continued. "What do you mean by *anomalous*?"

"You're a qualified lawyer and serious crime detective. I think you can work it out." Bone rolled his eyes.

The team fell silent for a moment, as though trying to readjust to their leader's return.

"Like, right now!" Bone bellowed.

"What about me?" Walker asked.

"We're off to see the counsel for the prosecution," Bone replied with a grimace.

After a flurry of phone calls to McLean's home and then his office, Bone and Walker discovered the advocate was chief prosecutor on a high-profile case at the High Court in Glasgow. When the two detectives arrived, the vast lobby area was abuzz with press and dodgy-looking visitors.

"It's the Sweeney brothers' case," Walker said.

Bone shrugged. "Who?"

"Gang wars. The Parkhead crime unit finally nailed the bastards, and the Sweeneys are up for extortion, kidnapping, torture, and murder."

"Not shoplifting, then," Bone said.

They pushed through the throng to the reception desk, where an immaculately suited young administrator was doing his best to ignore the noise. They flashed their IDs.

"We're looking for Chief Officer McLean," Bone said.

The receptionist smiled. "Everyone is after him," he said, his voice clipped.

"It's in connection with the disappearance of his wife."

The receptionist's face fell. "Oh, sorry, sir. Yes. I believe the session is about to recess for lunch. You may be able to catch him before he returns."

"Lunch? It's only half past ten," Bone said.

"The judge likes to take his time." The receptionist rolled his eyes, then glanced over his shoulder.

"Is he on the Sweeney case?" Walker asked.

"Of course, yes." The receptionist pulled another face. "I'll take you through to his chambers. This way, please."

After negotiating airport-style security, where the metal plate in Bone's head created a moment of panic with the machines, pushing the burly security guard to double-check his lanyard, the detectives followed the receptionist at pace through a labyrinth of high vaulted corridors lined with paintings of austere and stern-faced judges and lawyers from Scotland's high establishment past. Finally, the receptionist led them into a cavernous, mahogany panelled room, with a scattering of ostentatious antique furniture and lined from floor to ceiling with bookcases rammed with leather-bound volumes of legalese.

"Please wait here. He shouldn't be too long," the receptionist said and shut the door behind him.

"I hate these places, don't you? It's that smell I can't abide." Walker cringed.

"Camphorwood?" Bone asked.

"Wealth and privilege." Walker went over to examine the books.

Bone sat on one of the neatly upholstered regency chairs lined along the back wall. "A bit odd, wouldn't you say?"

"What?" Walker said, her finger about to pluck a book from the shelf, but then she changed her mind.

"McLean at work."

"It's a high-profile case, and if he's chief prosecutor…?"

"Yes, I know, but…"

Bone's thought was interrupted by the arrival of the Chief Officer, who swept into the room, dressed in full courtroom regalia, his gown trailing behind like Batman's cape. At first he didn't see them but then stopped. "Excuse me, this is a private office." And then he recognised Bone. "Inspector," he said, as though surprised to see him.

"Good morning, Mr McLean. You know DI Walker?"

McLean glanced over and nodded.

"We've come to talk about the disappearance of your wife," Bone could barely conceal his sarcasm.

"Yes, I know why you have come." McLean removed his wig and sat at his grandiose mahogany desk. "I told your superior that I have to be here today."

"Yes, we can see you have a very important case," Bone said, his anger growing.

"DCI Bone. This is a devastating nightmare," McLean snapped back. "But I have duties of the state and I am due back in court shortly. So do you have any news? Is she found yet?"

"No, but time is critical, and we are doing everything in our powers to find her."

"And there are links to the Meiklejohn case?"

"Not links, similarities," Bone replied.

"So no links," McLean repeated with a sigh.

"We need to establish what happened on the night of her disappearance." Bone ignored McLean's increasingly hostile tone.

The chief officer sifted through the papers and files in front of him. "I am extremely busy, DCI Bone. I fear we may lose this case, and that could be catastrophic for the criminal court system, not to mention the residents of Easterhouse."

Bone lost patience. "The grave threat to your wife is catastrophic, Mr McLean."

McLean stopped fidgeting and looked up. "I made it quite clear to your superior that I didn't want you anywhere near me. You are incompetent. You blew up a chief suspect and denied many grieving families the closure that they have lost forever."

"I think you'll find he blew me up," Bone said coldly.

McLean leaned back. "You have no *idea* how devastated I am. You think I'm here because I am cold and uncaring. It's a façade. This is my way of coping."

"We're just trying to find your wife, Mr McLean."

The man stood. "I have already given a statement to one of your uniformed officers. I have nothing more to add." He checked his watch. "Now if you'll excuse me, I'm due back in court."

McLean slotted his wig back in place, picked up a file from his desk, and with a flick of his gown, he headed for the door. Then he paused. "Find her," he said, before disappearing down the corridor.

Walker turned to Bone. "Bloody weird."

"Not what you'd call your usual response when your wife has been kidnapped," Bone agreed.

"Such a nice guy, though, isn't he?"

"Yes, I'd forgotten just how nice. I don't think we're quite done yet with PC Garvey's delightful husband." Bone said.

On the way back to Kilwinnoch, Walker's phone buzzed.

"Will?" she answered. "You'll need to speak up — we're in the DCI's car, and it's making the most horrendous sounds."

"Clutch," Bone shouted over the din. He crunched the gears again, and set off at a snail's pace through a set of lights as Walker listened to the call with a finger in her other ear.

A few moments later, she hung up. "Will's found something on the recording."

Bone put his foot down, with no apparent effect. He cursed loudly.

"You know we really should be using one of the pool cars," Walker said.

"I'm still technically on sick leave so I can drive whatever I like."

"That's what I'm worried about." Walker rolled her eyes.

The car spluttered, coughed, and rumbled on.

SIX

As the Saab approached the station, Walker spotted a small group gathered outside the entrance. "Looks like we have a fan club."

"Oh Christ," Bone replied. "How did they get wind?" He drove past the gaggle of reporters, photographers, and film crews, and parked up in the adjacent street. "Back door?" he asked.

They quickly crossed the street and shimmied through the rear gate.

"I'm going to bloody kill whoever's blabbed."

Entering the incident room, Bone was about to launch into a tirade when Harper approached.

"Sir. I think you need to see this," he said, adjusting his glasses manically.

Bone and Walker followed him to his desk. Clicking a few buttons, Harper woke the monitor.

"I'm using the force's editing app," he said.

The screen burst into life, and the snuff movie Bone had been sent started up.

"The app allows us to action capture, frame by frame, without distortion or loss of definition. It's pretty bloody smart." Harper flicked up his glasses again.

Bone leaned in closer.

"As I ran through the recording a second time, I spotted something interesting." He tapped his keyboard, and the images flicked forward. "Just about...here." He stopped the tape at the point where the digger was about to drop its second load. "There's a fraction of a second here where the camera angle changes. It's tricky because it's really fast."

Mullens and Baxter had joined them now, too, leaning in for a view of the screen. Harper tickled the still image, and it made a couple of minute movements.

"There!" he said triumphantly. "Can you see it?"

Bone stared at the image, but he couldn't make out anything different from the previous frames. Mullens' giant arm appeared over his head, and he spun round in surprise.

"That!" Mullens said, pointing at the top corner of the image.

Bone leaned in farther. The camera had caught a momentary glimpse of the corner of a steel girder. "Can you enhance that a bit more?"

Harper fiddled with the settings, and the image sharpened. It looked like part of a larger frame, a giant Meccano part.

"That's the new superstore they were building out at the old Langlands factory site," Mullens said.

Bone nodded. "Shit, you're right. But didn't Scotsave pull out or something?"

"Aye, I think the bungs weren't big enough, so the council blocked it, for now anyway."

"When was that?"

Mullens shrugged. "Not sure, to be honest, sir."

"Four months ago," Walker butted in. "Much to the joy of the local retailers and the frustrations of the developers."

"So who's in charge of the site now?"

"I think the supermarket has employed a security firm to guard the site at night, but it's just locked up in the day, I believe." Walker added.

Bone turned to Harper. "Can you print out that image?"

"Sure." Within a few seconds, an A4 copy emerged from the printer on the far side of the room. Harper dashed over, retrieved it, and handed it to Bone.

"Okay," Bone said. "Could someone call in a couple of squad cars and get the site sealed off? Mullens and Walker, you're with me."

"Sir, if I may, could I possibly accompany you?" Baxter asked. "I've been going through the Meiklejohn file all morning and I could really do with some fresh air. It's toxic stuff."

"Sorry, Sheila. I need you to carry on, I'm afraid."

Baxter blew out her cheeks.

"And stick anything you think might be important up on the board, got it?" Bone said, seeing the disappointment on her face.

Baxter nodded and reluctantly returned to the heap of files stacked up on her desk.

Bone picked up his coat. "Oh, and if you leave the station," he said, addressing the two desk jockeys, "use the back door as the vultures have landed. I'll deal with that later." On his way out, he shot a look at the coffee machine. "Bugger, I missed it again."

When Bone pulled up to the site gate, two police cars were already parked up, and three uniforms were milling around the entrance, the giant black steel skeleton looming ominously above. The detectives climbed out and approached.

Bone flashed his ID at one of the PCs.

"Morning, sir." The officer nodded.

A barn door of a man in a hi-vis jacket and hard hat appeared at the gate.

"I'm Detective Chief Inspector Bone. Are you the site foreman?"

"Davie Edmunson. I head up the groundworks team."

"Hello, Davie," Mullens cut in. "How's tricks?"

"Awright, Mark," the barn door replied.

"Is there anybody you don't know?" Bone raised an eyebrow at Mullens.

"Mr Popularity, me." Mullens grinned. "Davie's with R and G Groundworks — you know, the Lennoxfield crew."

"Aye. So what's the problem?" the foreman asked, scratching his head.

"I thought all work had stopped on the site?" Bone said.

"It has," Edmunson confirmed. "There's been some water-logging issues. The developer called us back in a couple of weeks ago to repair the drainage and reduce flooding."

Bone peered at the site. "So what size is your team?"

"We're on a reduced team at the minute. There's only the four of us."

"Were you all on site on Tuesday?"

"Last Tuesday?"

Bone nodded.

"Aye — no, wait," Edmunson paused. "We were only here in the morning — we had to vacate the site by twelve-thirty as Environmental Heath were planning to visit. Council sent us an email the day before about it, see?"

"So you locked up and left them to it?"

"No, they told me to leave the gate open and put the key in the site hut, and they would lock up when they left."

"Is the site guarded, or is there any CCTV?" Bone persisted.

"What for?" Edmunson shrugged. "There's bugger all here, and I don't think the scrap metal merchant would be that enamoured if some wee thieving ned turned up wae that lot." He glanced over at the uniforms milling around the frame. "So what's going on?"

"And did the council lock up after themselves?" Bone continued, ignoring him.

The foreman pulled a face. "I was late in on Wednesday. I'm no sure who was on site first. I'd need tae check that."

"Okay," Bone replied. "And now I'll need you to clear your team from the site."

"What — right now?"

"'Fraid so."

Edmunson sighed. "Okay. The boys won't be pleased, though, 'cos the office'll dock their pay. That's twice in one week. You'll be popular in the Fells tonight, Mark."

Mullens held up his hands. "Sorry, Davie. Needs must."

"I'll get the men and find out who opened up on Wednesday," Edmunson added. "It's no one of they gangland tit-for-tat killings, is it?"

"Is it okay if we come in with you and have a look around?" Bone ignored his question again.

"Aye, no bother. I'm warning you, though, it's a quagmire in there."

"Oh Jesus," Walker said, looking down at her gleaming Italian brogues.

"Say ta-ta to those puppies, Rhona," Mullens joked.

Bone unfolded the printouts he'd brought along and scanned them, his brow furrowing. He handed them to the two detectives. "Right, you two start at either end of Blackpool Tower; see if you can get a location match."

The detectives set off towards the structure while Bone followed the foreman along the track, past the frame, heading down to the perimeter fence. Glancing back, Bone spotted Mullens clambering over a pile of girders before stumbling forward and then disappearing. A moment later, he re-emerged, his roaring curse booming off the steel cage.

Once they had passed the forlorn abandoned skeleton, Bone spotted the crew at the fence, busy digging and shovelling around a mini excavator that scooped up buckets of muddy water and emptied it out a few feet away. As he and Edmunson approached, the path became muddier and muddier with stinking pools of murky filth on either side.

"Watch yer step here. Some of these holes would swallow a bus," the foreman warned.

When they reached the crew, the men downed tools and stared up in unison at Bone.

"Right, lads, the police are here," Edmunson announced. "They need us off the site. Get yer stuff."

The groundwork team groaned, reluctantly collected up their belongings, and then huddled together in front of the foreman.

"The inspector wants to know who was first on the site on Wednesday."

The crew all shot guilty looks at each other.

"Don't worry, it's not a trick question," Bone jumped in with a smile.

"I was," one of the young labourers said, his hand up as though he was still at school. "The gate was open, though." He glanced anxiously from the inspector to the foreman.

"And you didn't think to tell me that before?" the foreman said incredulously.

"Ah just thought that somebody was in before me." The young man shrugged.

"Who?" Bone asked.

"I dunno. I went straight into the site office."

"What were you doing in there?" the foreman demanded.

"Nothin'." The young lad shook his head. "I was just brewin' up. The kettle's in there."

"What's your name, son?" Bone asked.

"What d'you want ma name for?" the labourer shot back. "I wasn't doin' anything. I just made a brew and helped myself to one of Davie's ginger nuts."

The crew burst into laughter.

"That's the truth." A deep crimson flush crept across the lad's cheeks. "An' by the time I'd brewed up I'd forgot about the gate."

"So who else was in?" Edmunson pushed.

"Everybody, near enough."

"What's your name?" Bone repeated, this time firmly.

"It's Paul Quinn, biscuit thief," the foreman answered for the lad, shaking his head at him.

"And the Bobcat, do you keep that here overnight?"

"At the moment, aye," the foreman replied. "No point trailing it back and forth to our yard."

"So where's the key kept?"

The foreman looked at his crew. "Where do you keep it, John?"

John, a short, stout man with an unlit roll-up sticking out of his mouth, shrugged and mumbled some incoherent slur.

"Say whit?" the foreman said.

John removed the roll-up. "I said, the key's usually under the cab seat."

Bone blew out his cheeks. "Jesus. You wouldn't need to be storing the country's gold bullion supplies here. You need to sort out your security."

"We park up the digger out of sight under the frame," the foreman countered, jumping to the defence of his crew.

"And are you the digger man?" Bone asked John, who was now attempting to light his roll-up.

"Three of us here are licensed to operate it, but to be honest, it's not rocket science. With a couple of goes anyone could work it."

Bone glanced along the line of weary faces again. "Okay. That's all for now. Thanks for your help. Is it okay if we carry on here?"

"Aye, of course." The foreman nodded. "Right, lads, come on. Let the police do what they have to do, whatever that is."

"And on the way out can you all give your names to the PC on the gate?" Bone said, inciting a ripple of murmurs from the crew. He turned back to Edmunson. "I'm going to need to see that email from the council, too."

"Aye right, no bother."

Just then, a loud whistle rang out from the other side of the site.

Bone about-turned and headed towards Walker's signal.

"Bingo," she said, holding up her printout as Bone and then Mullens approached.

The image was a near perfect match with the scene directly ahead.

"The digger's been here." She pointed at some tracks in the mud that led to a clearing between two or three pallets stacked high with concrete blocks.

The trio clambered between the pallets to a ten-foot patch of freshly turned clay that stood out against the hard compacted surrounding soil.

"Oh shit. Looks like we're going to need a warrant," Walker said.

"And forensics." Bone sighed.

SEVEN

Bone left Mullens at the scene and drove Walker back to the station, dropping her on the corner of the street.

"Back door, I know," Walker said.

"Alert SOC and see if you can get permission from the council."

"Will do. Where are you going?" Walker asked.

"I've got something urgent that I need to attend to," Bonè said. He sped away with no further explanation, leaving Walker shaking her head.

Reaching his son's school, Bone pulled up at the far end of the road and checked his watch — still a few minutes to go before the bell rang for the end of the school day. He caught his reflection in the mirror and sighed. He looked terrible, there was no denying it. It had been a very long day already, and it showed. He quickly flattened down his somewhat deranged hair and jumped out. He stopped.

"Shoes. Shit." he glanced down at his mud-encrusted Docs, matched by equally dirty trouser hems. "Ah bugger it."

With a shrug he walked at a pace to the school entrance. A gaggle of noisy mums and dads were chatting. When they saw him approach, they stopped talking.

"Afternoon," Bone said. "I'm Michael Bone's dad, primary three." He didn't want them to think he was contemplating an abduction.

"Hey, Duncan," a voice at the back of the group pushed through. "How the devil are you?" the young man asked.

Bone studied the man's unshaven features, trying to place him.

"Alan Warnes, Craig's dad." It was clear the man knew that Bone was clueless as to his identity. "We met at Craig's birthday party last year," he added.

Bone was still none the wiser but pretended to remember. "Oh aye, that's right."

"How are you now anyway?" Alan asked.

"Oh fine, fine." Bone racked his brain for any nugget he could use to swerve the man's questions.

"That was terrible. What an evil bastard."

"Comes with the job. How's…" He'd already forgotten the boy's name.

"We're doing okay, but…you know." Alan pulled a face.

"Indeed," Bone agreed, but had no idea what the man meant.

"Are you back at work now?"

The clanging of the bell saved Bone from further discomfort, as the front doors of the school flew open and a tsunami of hobbits spilled out into the playground.

"Here they come." The young dad grimaced.

Bone scoured the ocean of grinning, shouting, sullen, and raspberry-blowing faces but couldn't see Michael.

A boy ran out through the gate and into Alan's arms.

The young dad scooped the boy up and ruffled his hair. "How's my wee toerag?"

"Fine," the boy answered. "Is Mummy here?"

"She's at work, but we're going to soft play."

The kid let out an excited yelp and jumped down onto the pavement.

"Well, it's good to see you, Duncan. Say hello to Alice for me." Alan smiled.

"Will do," Bone said. He waved at the boy as the pair walked off hand in hand.

Soon, most of the kids had been collected. After the last kid's mum had finally arrived, flustered and apologetic, and had bundled her wee girl into her car, Bone approached the teacher at the gate.

"Excuse me, I'm waiting for Michael Bone. I'm his dad."

"Oh hello, Mr Bone. It's lovely to meet you at last. I don't think we've met. I'm Felicity Swift, Michael's teacher." She held out her hand.

Bone briskly shook it.

She pulled it back to the safety of a pocket in her brightly coloured dress, fit for a production of *Joseph*. "I'm afraid Michael is off sick today."

"What's the matter?"

"I think his mum — sorry, your wife — said he had a temperature." She paused. "No, wait, that's Gillian Clarke, she's the one with the temperature." She looked at Bone, the greying streak at the front of her auburn hair flopping down over her eyes. "It's been one of those days." She smiled and pushed an errant lock of hair back to where it belonged. "Actually, it's always one of those days." The lock fell out again.

"Thanks." Bone hurried back up the street towards the car.

"It was nice to meet you…" she called out after him.

But Bone was already out of earshot.

When he reached his wife's front door, he poked at the buzzer repeatedly until he could hear her thumping down the hall.

"God's sake, where's the bloody fire?" she said, throwing the door open. "Oh, Duncan, it's you."

"What's happened?" Bone asked.

"What do you mean?"

"Michael," Bone returned quickly. "Why is he off school?"

"Oh, it's nothing. He just fell in the playground and cut his head. They sent him home as a precaution."

"Jesus. I thought something worse had happened!"

"Bloody hell, Duncan. Calm down. What's with the hysteria?"

"The school said he was off and — I don't know. It's been a really long, difficult day."

"Come in for a minute. He'll be pleased to see you." Alice ushered Duncan in and led him through to the living room.

Michael was propped up against a big cushion on the floor, his face almost in the TV, enjoying a cartoon.

"All right, wee fella?" Bone asked.

Michael turned round.

"Dad!" he squealed and, jumping to his feet, he clambered over the back of the sofa to reach him.

Bone plucked him up.

"Careful, Michael," Alice said.

"I hear you've been in the wars." Bone gave his son a big hug. "What's that on your head? Is it your brain poking out, aye?"

"A lump," Michael said proudly. "Barry Hutchison pushed me off the crazy castle."

"Did he now? Well, would you like me to go and arrest him?"

"Yes, please," Michael enthused.

"He's fine," Alice said. "Happy to be off school all day, aren't you, wee monkey?"

Michael nodded. "Are you going to stay?"

"Here to see how my wee soldier's doing." Bone smiled and tickled him. "Though I think he might be milking it a wee bit."

Michael laughed uncontrollably and then let out a loud fart. He stopped, and then they all laughed together.

"Okay, Michael, your dad wants a cup of coffee. You go back to your cartoon for a bit, and you can speak to him in a while," Alice said.

Bone slid Michael back down onto the sofa, returning the boy to his front-row cushion by the TV before following Alice into the kitchen.

"You look like shit, Duncan."

"Aw, thanks." Bone winked.

"Has your PTSD been bad today? Is that why you're panicking?" She picked up the kettle and started filling it.

"No, not at all."

"Have you had anything to eat? I bet you haven't."

"I'm back at work," Bone cut in.

"What?" Alice turned off the tap. "Tell me you're joking."

"I think it's time."

"I can't believe this."

"There's a new case. They need me."

"There's always a new bloody case." She slammed the kettle down hard onto its base, then flicked the switch. "You said over and over you were done with it."

"I'm climbing the walls in that flat."

"And this is all okay with your rehab team and your counsellor? They think you're fit for duty?" She shook her head in disbelief.

"Gallacher is happy for me to come back." Bone dodged her question.

"I bet he bloody is." She spooned some coffee into a mug.

"Listen, Alice…" He moved towards her. "Being off sick wasn't helping me anymore. I'm a police officer, it's all I know. I can't do anything else. And if I give it up, I'm frightened I'll be a basket case for the rest of my life."

"Do what you like," Alice snapped.

"I'm a better person when I'm working, and I really am on the mend."

She sighed. "I'm not sure I am, though."

"Maybe once you get used to this and I can show you that the wheels are definitely back on, then you might consider letting me see Michael a bit more." He paused and then added, "And you?"

"Hold on." She raised her hands.

"Sorry, I shouldn't have sprung it on you like that. Maybe if I get my counsellor to ring you and reassure you?"

"You put us through hell. *You* were hell."

"Just cut me some slack, Alice — please," Bone said. "I just want to be a dad to my wee boy."

Alice sighed, refusing to look at him.

"I can't pretend that the PTSD is gone completely, but it doesn't control me like it did. I'm not angry or scared of it anymore. I just thought I could maybe start seeing him more regularly, maybe once a week or something like that. I could drop him or pick him up after school, and he could stay over once in a while? I can help now."

"Stop," Alice interrupted. "Just back up a bit."

Bone stepped away, confused.

67

"No, I didn't mean… Anyway, let's see how it goes, okay; let's see how *you* go?"

"Does that mean I can see Michael?"

"Let's just think about what's best for him and we'll see."

"I think he needs his dad." Bone sensed another of her *nos* coming on.

"I don't want to get into it tonight, Duncan. Why don't you go and say cheerio to him, and then I'll ring you, okay?"

Bone sensed she was stalling. "I just want to be a part of his life again."

Alice pushed past him and returned to the living room.

"Your dad's going now, Michael," she said.

Bone went over and picked him up again for a cuddle.

"Bye, Dad." Michael made a sad face.

Bone mimicked his expression. "I'll see you soon, lumpy heed, okay?"

Michael threw his arms round Bone's neck and squeezed tightly.

He unpeeled his son and lowered him down, the boy still clinging to his legs.

"What's this you're watching?" Bone asked, and picked up the remote to distract him.

"*Space Ninjas*," Michael replied, zoning in on the cartoon.

Bone sat on the floor beside him.

"I could take him out, no bother." He shouldered his boy playfully.

"He's got a laser arm and he would zap you," Michael replied, his eyes glued to the screen.

"My bionic arm is stronger," Bone said and, clenching his fist, he play-punched Michael on the cheek in slow motion.

Michael swerved and, raising his arm, blasted his dad with an imaginary ray gun. Bone toppled sideways, feigning a hit.

"Okay, Michael. Let your dad go," Alice said, shaking her head.

Bone stood, brushed the top of his son's head with his hand, and then left the boy there, mouth agape, as a giant cyclops fired deadly beams at a samurai sword-wielding, half-naked frog.

"Go home and eat something," Alice said from the door.

"I meant what I said," Bone replied.

"I know you did. This is a big deal. Let's just see what happens."

"Okay," Bone agreed, finally recognising the need to back off. "Call me, please."

She nodded and shut the door. After a moment, Bone retreated down the path, the sound of the ray gun booming through the closed door.

EIGHT

By the time Bone got home, it was already dark. He'd anticipated his first day back to be full-on but not on this monumental scale. He dropped his bag on the floor and checked his answerphone. No messages. He let out a long, weary sigh of relief, and shuffling through to his pokey galley kitchen, opened the fridge in search of food. One half-eaten, mouldy tomato and a desiccated mushroom staring back at him. He slammed the door shut and checked the barren wasteland of his top cupboard, hoping for a tin of soup. Nothing.

Bugger. Returning to the living room, he sifted through a small collection of LPs stacked up on the floor by an age-worn Dansette record player. He plucked out a record and loaded it up on the turntable. As the arm clicked and the needle dropped, he slumped down on the sofa and let out a sigh. Billie Holiday's near broken but beautiful rendition of *'Sleepy Time Down South'* spilled into the room. Bone closed his eyes and let Holiday's soothing, plaintive voice wash over and through him.

He felt himself slowly sink into her comforting, familiar arms, just as the doorbell rang, shaking him out of his momentary solace. The bell sounded again.

"Oh dear God," he complained. With a groan, he pulled himself up and went to answer it.

"Hi," said Walker, who was standing before him, clutching a pizza box. "Sorry to disturb you, sir. I was just passing, and I thought you'd want to know that Baxter cleared access with the council and the CSI team are on the scene now. We should know one way or another in a few hours."

"You could have told me that on the phone," Bone said.

"And I figured you'd probably be in need of this." She smiled and held up the pizza box.

Bone chuckled. "Perfect timing. It's like the potato famine in here. Come in."

"I don't want to intrude."

"Oh shut up." Bone grinned.

She followed him in.

"I see you're still listening to your old man's record collection," Walker said as they entered the living room.

"He might have been a seriously flawed human being, but he had bloody good taste in music." Bone opened a sideboard and, digging around, removed a flat cardboard container. "Did I ever show you this?" From the end of the box he carefully removed an LP.

"What is it?" Walker put the pizza box down on the dining table.

"This is an original acetate pressing of *Kind of Blue*."

Walker shrugged.

"You don't know *Kind of Blue*?"

Walker shrugged again.

"Miles Davis, Jesus!" Bone exclaimed. "One of the greatest and most influential pieces of music ever written, by a complete nutjob." He handed it to her.

"I'm more of a Runrig kinda person." She turned it over.

"Are they even still going, and if so, why?" Bone grimaced.

"It's signed!" Walker looked up in surprise.

"Not only that, but when my dad died, and I discovered it in his loft, I found a letter inside the sleeve, from the man himself addressed to my old man. It's up there on the wall." He pointed at the frame above the Dansette.

Walker went over to read it. "Wow, that's something. He must have been good mates with this Davis guy."

"You are pulling my chain, aren't you?"

"I really haven't heard of him."

"Philistine."

"How did he know him, then?"

"That's still a mystery. He never mentioned it to me or my mother, or anyone else as far as I know. He probably supplied him with some class A," he joked.

"You should get a decent detective on to that. I might know someone who could help you."

"Very funny." Bone scoffed, carefully returning the acetate to its box.

"Must be worth a bit, though, if this is the masterpiece you say it is?"

"Priceless and not for sale." The smell of pepperoni filled Bone's nostrils. "Are we going to eat this or what?"

"I didn't get a chance to say it earlier — it's good to have you back. But I also just wanted to check you're okay. It wasn't exactly a relaxing, gentle return to work," Walker said, lifting the lid of the pizza box.

"I'll get some plates." Bone ignored her question and wandered off to the kitchen.

When he came back, Walker opened up a small rucksack and pulled out a bottle of red.

"I thought you might be needing something a bit stronger," she said, putting the bottle down in front of him.

"You know, I've not really touched the sauce since the accident," Bone said.

"Sorry, I didn't mean to…" She went to grab the bottle.

"Leave it," he interjected. "I think it's time I jumped down off that wagon." He unscrewed the top and poured two large glassfuls.

Walker took off her coat and hung it on the back of her chair.

Laying out the plates, Bone helped himself to a slice.

"Ladies first," Walker joked.

"I'm bloody starving," Bone mumbled through his already stuffed mouth. "So how's Maddie?"

"She's fine. Still teaching and still dreaming of becoming that successful writer."

"It'll happen," Bone said. "She's just got to keep at it, and don't let the bastards grind her down."

"Christ, I hope it does. You think our paperwork's bad? Jesus, what a shit job teaching is."

"So no church bells yet?"

"God no, but we are thinking of adopting."

"Well, that's fantastic." Bone grinned. "I've always thought you two would make great pet owners."

"Very funny." She sighed. "I'm still not sure, though. I mean, I'm always at the station, staring at mutilated corpses, and she's a slave to the state. How's it going to work?"

"Ach, away with you. You two'll be fantastic parents. Do it — that's an order." Bone took a large gulp of wine. "That tastes bloody good," he said, enjoying a second mouthful.

They both fell into silence, munching their meal. After a few moments, Walker dropped her half-eaten slice onto her plate.

"You know, McLean's behaviour is bugging me."

"How so?" Bone asked sarcastically.

"This was not a guy in shock or in pieces. He was more concerned about his court case than his missing wife. And aside from being a number one arrogant arsehole, it was also extremely unprofessional of him to attack you in that way."

"I hear what you're saying, but like he said, I think it could be his way of coping."

"What, to be a number one prick?"

"Trauma affects people in different ways. But once a prick always a prick, especially in a crisis." Bone started on a third slice.

Walker shrugged. "Maybe you're right."

"Remember how he was before, when we were building a case against Meiklejohn. He was a difficult and conceited sod then. Grief just overinflates good and bad personality traits."

Walker picked at her pizza. "The other thing that's annoying me—" She stopped short. "Sorry, I'm talking shop. That's probably the last thing you want to do."

"Well, you're here now. Fill your boots and your face." Bone smiled.

"How does this copycat have so much inside knowledge of the Meiklejohn case? Peek-a-boo's father has got to be in the frame here, right?" She wiped the grease from her hand with her other hand.

"Maybe. Hold on." Bone disappeared into the hall and returned with a toilet roll.

"Wow, classy."

"Pretend you're camping. That's what I do." Bone sniggered. "He's sixty-nine and not exactly match fit. I'm not sure he'd have the physical strength to haul Garvey's body about."

"An accomplice then, or he confided in someone?"

"Possibly. He's not off the Christmas card list, that's for sure. My worry is if we are dealing with an obsessive fan, then this could escalate very quickly."

"That's usually how it works." Walker frowned.

"I think that's why Gallacher wanted me back. He knows where this could be heading."

"He wanted you back because he knows how good you are. But don't tell my boss I told you that, he's unbearable enough as it is." She stopped chewing on a crust. "God, this is shite, sorry."

"Didn't notice. My stomach was doing all the eating."

"He didn't pressure you into coming back then?" she continued. "I mean, are you sure you're okay? This case is pretty much bang on the knuckle of the bastard psycho who put you in the hospital."

"It's good to be back." Bone nodded reassuringly. "Most of that shit I was going through has gone now. I was ready to return. I needed to for my own sanity."

"That's good to hear. Anytime you need to shout or swear, you know where I am."

"I know, and I'm sorry I just dropped off the radar. I think I needed to go to the farthest place so that I could find my way back. That probably doesn't make any sense."

"Nope." Walker grinned.

When she had finished her wine, she set the glass down and stood. "Listen, I'll leave you to it. I'm sure you're champing at the bit to throw me out."

"The thought had crossed my mind."

At the door, Walker turned. "So SOC will probably call this in at three or four a.m. I'll go if you like."

"No, it's my watch. You get your beauty sleep."

"You look like the one in more need of that, you cheeky bastard," she replied.

"Thanks for the pizza and the company." And with a farewell smile, he shut the door.

He sank back against the frame, his body screaming at him to go and lie down. He quickly cleared away the dishes, locked up, and retreated to bed. If the forensics team were going to wake him in a few hours, he would need to get some kind of head start.

He lay down on top of the duvet, to gather his strength before undressing. But in the blink of a moment, he was fast asleep.

A whispering voice pulled him up from the depths of deep slumber. "Peek-a-boo."

He opened his eyes, his head pounding like a storm. The hooded apparition had returned, its grotesque, malformed features a hair's breadth from his cheek. He jerked back, instinctively throwing another defensive fist. The hallucination slid back across the room and settled in the dark recesses of the farthest corner. Bone rubbed at his eyes and peered into the gloom. The creature was upright, its pit-black form reaching almost as high as the ceiling.

"You're in my head. Fuck off!" Bone cried out. Grasping for his shoe by the side of the bed, he lobbed it into the shadows. The shoe bounced off the wall and dropped to the floor.

The apparition seemed to sink a little lower and it moved closer.

"What do you want?" Bone asked, though not sure why.

"Peek-a-boo," it whispered again.

"Meiklejohn?" Bone snarled.

The shadow rushed towards him. Bone threw up his hands to protect himself, but when he opened his eyes, the apparition had vanished.

"Jesus Christ," Bone cursed. He checked the bedside clock. 3:45 a.m. He got up and searched for his mobile. Thanks to the unwelcome lodger squatting in the depths of his brain, sleep was now an impossible dream.

NINE

The recovery team had been busy since his last visit to the site. There was a cordon around the perimeter, and then once inside the gate, a second surrounded the crime scene. Four sets of football league-sized floodlights had been installed, the stark white LEDs making the scene look like something out of a sci-fi movie. When Bone stumbled across the muddy path to the second cordon, a PC stopped him.

Bone produced his ID. "How's it going in there?"

"Bloody gruesome," the PC replied.

Bone lifted the tape, but the PC stopped him.

"Sir, you'll have to wear these." The PC handed him a set of disposable overshoes.

Bone sighed, wrestled them on over his Docs, and limboed under the tape. He approached the epicentre of the crime scene. The SOC team bobbed in and out of a deep wound in the ground, their white Teletubby suits glowing under the bright LED lights. Bone spotted a familiar face emerging from a tent erected on the far side of the crater. Andrew Cash, chief forensic officer at SOC, and known to most in the squad as 'the man in black', gave Bone a wave and picked his way towards him.

"Well, look what the cat dragged in," he said as he neared, his greying, unkempt locks peeking out of the hood of his tie-top bin bag. "I didn't know you were back."

"Yesterday."

"Starting as you mean to go on, I see?" Cash sighed.

"So, what have you found?"

"We excavated the area. That took forever, trying not to disturb or contaminate the scene, which of course is bloody impossible. But we got there in the end, and sadly we unearthed a deceased female body approximately three metres down."

They walked over to the edge of the crater. Bone peered down. Two forensic officers knelt by a body, half-submerged in the mud. One was taking photographs, the flash momentarily illuminating the deceased's mud-spattered, duct-taped head.

"She's been dead for some time. A few days — my guess is three," Cash continued. "We also recovered a police lanyard. It looks like we've found Police Constable Garvey."

"Shit." Bone muttered and leaned farther over the crater. "Can I get a bit closer?"

"You can but you'll have to don the romper."

"Pass." He sidled a little farther along the crater's edge, almost slipping in. "These fucking foot condoms. How can you work in them?"

"Practice. Just be careful. We don't want you falling in and soiling evidence."

"Charming." He slid as close as he could get and knelt.

The half-submerged body was lying at an odd angle, twisted into an extreme 'S' shape, the head sitting at a near ninety degrees to the shoulder, and one leg almost turned in on itself.

"What's that about?" Bone asked.

"Most likely caused by the compaction of soil, or possibly death throes."

"Nice."

"Not the best way to die, that's for sure." Cash puffed. "Death is such a sorry state of affairs," he added in his customary existential manner, staring for a moment in dark contemplation at the crumpled body in the hole. "I've got to go." He shook himself out of it. "We'll know more when we get the body back to the examination centre."

"Okay," Bone said.

He turned back to PC Garvey's terrible remains. A blackened and lifeless eye peeked out from a hole cut in the tape, her accusatory gaze staring directly at him. He pulled back from the edge and, clambering away from the woman's premature muddy grave, he began the grim process of working out how he was going to break the news to McLean.

TEN

Mullens was late for work, as usual, but this morning his tardiness was compounded by Bone ordering an early start. He stuffed a triple-decker cheese-and-jam toastie in his mouth, grabbed his coat, and at the door leaned over to kiss Sandra, his half-the-size wife, goodbye. She thumped his shoulder.

"No with that hangin' out yer mouth, ya dafty," she said, snatching it out of his jaws, a torn chunk of bread still clinging to his teeth. She landed him a big sloppy one in among the medley of dairy condiments.

"Now bugger off and earn some money, ya big lazy arse." She smiled, then stopped him. "What's that?" She pointed at his bulging coat pocket.

"My morning joy at gazing upon your Amazonian physique, dearest love of my life."

"Let me see." She grappled with his shovel-sized hands for a moment, but he pulled away. "Okay, okay, it's a mid-morning snack," Mullens admitted.

Sandra shook her head. "I swear you've got tapeworms the size of tube trains growing in there."

When he reached the car, he'd almost totalled the toastie, but while searching for his keys, he accidentally dropped the last crust on the ground. He reached down, picked it up, and snaffled it. He was about to get in the car when his wife appeared at the door, waving frantically.

He mouthed a "what?", but she waved at him to come back. Shaking his head and checking his watch, he reluctantly returned.

"What?" he repeated.

"Yer dad's just phoned," Sandra said.

"Oh no!" Mullens moaned. "Whit's up now?"

"He said there's some kinda intruder in his garden."

"What sort of intruder?"

"I dunno. You're the bloody detective. An intruder. Somebody trying to break in."

Mullens sighed. "Oh, please don't tell me you told him I'd call round on my way to work?"

"I told him you'd call round on your way to work." She grinned.

"Aw, Sandra!" Mullens complained. "I'm already late."

"Aw, Sandra, nothin'. He's yer dad and he sounded feart, if truth be told. I don't think it's nonsense this time."

"He should just phone the police. They'll be round in two shakes."

"Mark. You *are* the police. Come on, he's no long lost his wife. He's on his own and gets spooked."

"But why is it always when I'm at work? I'd be more than happy to help…" He stopped. "Wait, he's a complete pain in the arse, and I'd rather go diving in a septic tank."

"So shall I ring him to say you're on your way?"

"Aye, but Bone's going to rip me a new butthole!"

"Yer dadda's wee boy, aren't you?" She reached up and pinched his cheek.

He brushed her arm away and marched back to his car. As he got in, Sandra blew him a sarcastic kiss, and he gave her the finger. Their neighbour, Janice McIlroy, who was cleaning her front window — a daily occurrence which facilitated her role as the street's self-ordained busybody — spotted his gesture and pulled a face. Mullens blew her a kiss, and she lowered her blinds. As he drove off, his dad's message played on his mind, and in light of what was going on at the station, his worries escalated. He needed to be there fast. He put his foot down, and the souped-up pool car responded with an impressive growl.

His dad's 1930's council house was located at the more respectable end of the Northlands estate. Mullens parked up and dashed through the small overgrown garden to the door and, fumbling with his spare key, he opened up.

"Da, it's me," he called out, scanning the hallway.

No reply.

"George?" Mullens tried again, the panic rising in his chest.

"In here," a voice called from the living room.

Mullens dashed in. "What's going on? Are you okay?" He approached his old man, who was slumped as usual in his moth-eaten support chair. "Sandra said there's somebody trying to break in?"

"I've nae signal," his dad replied.

"What?"

"On that. Nae picture." He pointed accusingly at the TV directly in front of him.

"What about the intruder?"

"He's still oot there."

"Where?" Mullens squinted through to the kitchen.

George picked up the stick that was resting on his chair and brandished it like a sword. "I'll fuckin' have him."

"Who? You're not making sense."

"Him!" George jabbed the stick at the back door.

Mullens looked again and spotted a figure moving past the kitchen window.

"Shite!" Mullens cried and dashed into the kitchen, fists raised. He was about to lunge out the back door when the figure reappeared on the other side of the fence.

"Oh, for fuck's sake!" Mullens muttered.

It was his dad's next door neighbour, Bill Shannon, angrily pacing up and down on his own side of the fence.

Mullens returned to the living room, relieved but a little crestfallen that the services of his fists were no longer required. "Da, that's your neighbour, Bill."

"Who?"

"For the love of…" Mullens impatience was now getting the better of him. "Bill Shannon, next door. He's not even in your garden. Have you two had a barney again?"

"Nope." The old man shifted his huge bulk from one side of his support chair to the other as its creaking frame listed like the *Titanic* shortly after impact.

"Bloody hell, Da. I thought you were in trouble."

"I am in trouble. I have no TV."

Mullens sighed and marched out the back to handle his dad's neighbour.

"Mr Shannon," Mullens called over, and girded his loins for a verbal onslaught.

"Good morning, Mark. I'm glad you're here. Your dad was out earlier." Mr Shannon pulled the cord in his dressing gown tighter.

"Dad was out? You mean out-out, *outside* out?"

"Indeed."

"But how?"

"Another miracle of modern medicine? I don't know, but…" Mr Shannon gestured for Mullens to follow him along the side of the fence, back to the narrow space between the two houses. "I heard an almighty crash and came running out to find this."

He pointed below his side of the fence, and Mullens leaned over. A satellite dish was embedded in Mr Shannon's cloche, while smashed glass and the broken wooden frame were strewn all over his veg patch.

"Oh God, so sorry, Bill," Mullens said, glancing up at the trashed bracket and dangling cables on the side of his dad's house, where the dish used to live. "How the hell did he manage that?"

"Must be all those drugs they give him. He'll be turning green soon and terrorising the whole town, instead of just me." Bill sniffed.

"I'll pay for the damage, of course."

"Well, that's kind of you. But it'll take more than money for my prize marrow to win the harvest fair now."

Mullens looked back at the dish. The soggy remnants of the obliterated vegetable oozed out from under the rim.

"I can't apologise enough for the total liability that is my father. But listen, I've got to go to work now, so would it be okay if I dig that out of there tonight?"

"Tell George the next time he can't get *Homes Under the Hammer* on his telly, to leave it to the experts, okay?" Mr Shannon stomped back to his house.

Back inside, George was still fiddling with the remote.

"Okay, Dad, how did you do it?"

"Whit?" his dad said innocently, randomly pressing buttons.

Mullens snatched it out of his hands. "How did you knock the satellite dish off your wall and propel it with force into your neighbour's greenhouse?"

"It's no a greenhoose. It's that stupid thing."

"How?"

"Well, the TV wisnae workin'. I tried everything and then I went out to check the dish."

"And how did you manage to get out on your own?"

"I used that," George said, pointing accusingly at a Zimmer frame upended in his bedroom doorway.

"You used your frame?"

"Well, it was an emergency. I mean, I was gonnae miss my programme."

"Okay, so you went out and—?"

"I just tapped it a wee bit."

"Tapped it? What with, a JCB bucket?"

"Wae the washin' line pole."

"Jesus Christ."

"Just a wee nudge."

"Dad, you launched it halfway into Bill's garden."

"I was missin' ma programme." George shook his head.

"Oh God, right. I'll get it fixed. In the meantime, you'll just have to watch Freeview."

"It's all a load of pish on that."

"It's exactly the same load of pish you usually watch except not via Rupert Murdoch's wallet."

Mullens dug the Freeview box out from under his dad's stairs and plugged it in for him.

"Right. I'll leave you with this."

He handed him a second remote, but his dad continued to press the first.

"I give up," Mullens complained. "I'll be back after ma shift, okay, and retrieve the *USS Enterprise* from Bill's garden."

George nodded but was too busy now wrestling with both remotes.

"And remember, there's always a book or the radio?"

"Load of pish," his dad huffed.

Mullens left him to it.

ELEVEN

When Bone reached the station, the sun was coming up. The gaggle of news hounds had shrunk to a small huddle of hardcore hacks. Someone was going to have to speak to them, and as it was quiet, this was probably the least painful opportunity. He parked the car opposite the station and strode towards the entrance. One or two reporters spotted him approaching and the group sprang to life, dropping half-full coffee cups, snatching at cameras and notepads, and setting upon him like a swarm of malevolent bees. Bone spotted Colin McKinnon, the staff reporter for *The Chronicle* and long-time gorse bush up his arse. The questions came in rapid succession as competing journalists tried to trump their rivals.

"What can you tell us about the crime scene out at the Langlands superstore site?"

"Has there been a murder?"

Then McKinnon stuck his face in front of the jostling rabble. "Has the Peek-a-boo Killer struck again, DCI Bone?"

The journalists stopped wrestling with each other for a moment and tuned in to Bone's response.

"We are conducting an investigation out at Langlands construction site. At this stage, I have nothing more to add," Bone said.

"Has Peek-a-boo struck again?" McKinnon persisted.

Bone turned on him. "Fact check, Mr McKinnon. Meiklejohn, the so-called Peek-a-boo Killer, is dead."

"Is he, though? That's what anxious residents of Kilwinnoch will want to know. Are we safe in our beds?"

"Residents are in no immediate danger and need not be alarmed," Bone growled at McKinnon.

"Did you hunt down an innocent man, DCI Bone?"

"Like I said, we've nothing further to add at this stage of our inquiries." Bone pushed through the group, taking the station steps two at a time and dashing through the door.

"Fucking cockroach," he snarled.

"Who's that?" Sergeant Brody asked from the desk, furtively dropping a half-eaten sausage roll onto the plate in front of him.

"That *Chronicle* reporter. He's worse than a case of toe fungus, and that paper he writes for is just as bad."

"Aye, I know," Brody folded up his copy and pushed it under a ledger.

"Whatever you do, don't let that vermin in, okay?"

"Shoot to kill." Brody smirked.

Bone thought he'd be first in, but Baxter was already at her desk.

"You're up early, Detective," Bone said, removing his coat.

Baxter stretched and yawned. "Morning sir. I couldn't sleep. Have they found PC Garvey?"

"Looks like it. I've just been over there. Forensics are on it now."

"So tragic. It's very upsetting."

"It is that." Bone set his bag down by his desk. "How did you get on with Advocate McLean?"

"Well, as you would expect, a glowing record of high-profile success. Over the years he's put away quite a few heavy-duty criminals, killers, and first-class scum bags."

"So plethora of enemies." Bone frowned.

"Indeed, and not all in the criminal fraternity."

"What d'you mean?"

"He's had some headline-making run-ins with a number of successive governments and the law-making establishment. He appears to have plenty to say about quite a lot of things."

"Aye, well, that comes as no surprise."

"But in the last few months he's not been winning quite as many cases as he used to. He seems to be on something of a losing streak; not a good place to be when you've been flying from a great height and shitting on those beneath you."

"Indeed." Bone made a beeline for the coffee machine.

Half an hour later, Mullens rumbled in, almost taking the door off its hinges.

"Fuckin' three-ring circus out there!" he moaned, throwing his coat at the stand. It missed the peg. "Sorry I'm late, domestic crisis."

"Your dad again?" Baxter asked.

"Who else?"

"I hope you didn't say anything to that shower of parasites out there," Bone said.

"Other than unbroadcastable instructions on what they can do with their mics, not a peep."

"How did you get on yesterday at the Fells?"

"Hold yer horses, Herr Kapitan," Mullens grumbled. He retrieved his coat from the floor and from his bulging pocket produced a triangle of pizza loosely wrapped in a kitchen towel. He proceeded to devour it like a lion feasting on an antelope's liver.

"Jesus, Mark," Bone said, both awed and disgusted at the same time.

"Waste not, want not." Mullens rammed his face farther into the now sodden wrapper. "Interesting trip to the Fells," he mumbled through mouthfuls. "They've stopped the half-price breakfast baps, bloody shocking."

"Did you speak to the landlord?"

"Aye, I did that, and I told Big Andy he was on a loser dropping the offer."

"DS Mullens!" Bone cut in.

"So, anyways…" Mullens wiped his face on the sleeve of his suit jacket. "Andy said that apart from the polis party, the bar was quiet that night, and I did point out that was probably due to his regulars takin' a huffy about his scroogin' change of heart with his bacon bap offer."

"Proceed!"

"So, he remembered big Dougie Drysdale comin' in for his usual vat of Dutch courage before venturing home, but he left before the party got started. Ron the Rake was in, and also Big whatshisface Dobson, you know, who used to run the bike shop."

"Derek Dobson, is it?"

"Dunno, I've always called him Big Dobber, but it doesn't seem that appropriate now he's seventy-two. He was in until about nine, he thinks, and he left before Garvey. But the big name that was in that stoked my boiler was John Meiklejohn." He looked up. "I mean, what dunderheid of a parent would name their wean John when their second name's Meiklejohn?" He shook his head.

"The father?" Bone asked, trying to keep Mullens on message.

"Aye, so it appears. Andy said he was in for a few hours and he had to stop serving him because he was so blootered."

"Well, now. Did Andy remember when he left or if he was anywhere near Garvey?"

"Didn't say anything about speaking to Garvey, and he wasn't exactly sure when Meiklejohn left the pub, but he thinks maybe just before the polis party cleared out. He said he was so busy trying to get rid of him, he didn't notice the Campsie coppers leave."

"So does he regularly frequent the Fells?"

Mullens shrugged. "Not to my knowledge, though I'm not in there that often either." He glanced up at the team guiltily.

"Aye, righto." Bone shook his head.

"Seriously, though, I can't remember the last time I saw him in there, but he's barred from most drinking holes in the town, so he might have been tryin' his luck."

"Possibly," Bone replied.

"Aw, sir, there's just no way. I mean, he's an alky. He couldn't do this. He doesn't have the brains, the health, or the strength."

"Maybe not directly, but he's a drunk because of what happened to his son."

"Nah, he was a loser drunk before then. His son is just an excuse to plough on."

"Sir?" Baxter interrupted.

"Aye?" Bone spooned some coffee into the percolator.

"You told me to run a few checks on the groundworks team that were on site yesterday."

Bone nodded, fiddling with the switch.

"Oh, sorry, sir. I finished what was in there from last night and forgot to refill it."

"That's no problem, Baxter. I would have been shocked to my core if you hadn't snaffled it." Bone smiled. "Anyway, the groundworks team?"

"Yes, well, I've just found something." She tapped her screen. "One of the labourers on the list, a Paul Quinn?"

"Aye, he was the numpty who arrived on the site first."

"Seven years ago, he was working on a labouring job at Gatehouse of Fleet, some big motorway upgrade. He was employed by Baird Construction."

"The big guns."

"That's right. He was part of a subcontracted landscaping team."

"And?"

"It turns out that our friend, a Mr Robert Meiklejohn, was employed on the same contract."

"Is that right?"

"There's more," Baxter continued. "It transpires that they were living and working on the site together for about six weeks."

"So in shared accommodation?"

"I would assume so. I mean, it could be a complete coincidence…" Baxter raised her eyebrow.

"No such thing in our game. Let's bring him in for questioning."

"Shall I do that?"

"No. Check through Meiklejohn Senior's record. I know he's had plenty of past scrapes with the law, but see if he's been a naughty boy recently."

"What am I looking for?"

"Copycat murder would be a good start." The percolator gurgled, and Bone half-filled a cup with the first dribbles of coffee, stirring in two heaped spoonfuls of sugar and then downing it in one. He had a feeling it was going to be another very long day.

TWELVE

Bone called ahead to the Campsie Fells Station to request interviews with PC Garvey's party colleagues. The desk sergeant wasn't sure who was on duty but would try his best to round them up. Bone then called Walker to tell her to meet him there.

Frank Gilbert, the DCI at the station, was what most locals would affectionately call a first-class fud. Bone had known Gilbert as far back as police training, when Gilbert had bored all and sundry with his tall tales of female conquests and how it was 'his divine destiny' to be Scotland's chief constable. Luckily for womankind and the force, his plague-rat personality had managed to both limit his choice of eligible women to zero, and his promotional aspirations to the DCI of a backwater nick — in Bone's mind, a position already too high up the food chain.

Inside the station, the friendly desk sergeant greeted the two detectives, and Gilbert made his appearance shortly after. Bone hadn't seen Gilbert for a couple of years, and the passage of time had not been kind. The DCI had acquired something of a

Michelin tyre set around his midriff, along with a rather alarmingly voluptuous pair of moobs, which pressed ominously against his shirt.

"Duncan, always a joy," Gilbert smarmed.

"Likewise," Bone replied, unable to rein in his sarcasm.

"Surprised to see you back so soon after such devastating injuries," Gilbert said. "I thought you'd pegged it there for a tick."

"Still ticking. You look well," Bone lied.

"Ach, away with you. I'm out of shape. I need to get back on a treadmill." Gilbert touched his gut briefly then glanced over at Walker. "And who is your charming colleague?"

"DI Walker, sir. But if you're looking for charm, I suggest a visit to the nineteen seventies." Walker frowned.

Bone concealed a smile.

Gilbert stared at her for a moment, seemingly unsure how to respond, then with an embarrassed cough, he ushered the detectives through. "Terrible business, and so distressing for Mr McLean," he said, finally finding his voice. "PC…" He paused.

"Garvey," Bone replied impatiently.

"Yes, PC Garvey was a such a huge asset to the station and the force, and so well liked by everyone."

His insincere platitudes fell on deaf ears as the three of them continued to the end of a narrow corridor, where Gilbert stopped by a door.

"I've set you up in here."

Bone and Walker followed him into a claustrophobically small room, its walls painted in sickly pastel colours and furnished with cheap sub-IKEA pieces and what professionals would call 'quiet lighting.' The type of hideous space Bone was more than familiar with.

"This is a bereavement room," Bone said.

"Yes, that's right. I thought…"

"Not in here," Bone interrupted. "I need the PC's colleagues to be fit for interview, not blubbering emotional wrecks."

"I just thought it might be more conducive."

"To what, a funeral?" Bone snapped back. "I need answers and clear heads, not cops in the mood for a wake." He turned to go. "An interview room will be fine."

"As you wish," Gilbert huffed.

They returned to the corridor, and Gilbert marched Bone and Walker through a set of double doors, down a flight of stairs, and into another room, this time with bare concrete walls, a table, four chairs, and a tape recorder.

"Well if you're sure about this?" Gilbert asked.

"Positive." Bone settled himself into a chair and folded his arms.

"The PC's colleagues are waiting in the staff canteen. Shall I send them in one at a time?"

"Yes, thank you."

"Would you like a cup of coffee or anything?"

Bone looked up and smiled. "Whisky, if you have it."

Gilbert huffed again. "I'm not sure we're—"

"I'm joking. A coffee's fine. Black, two sugars." Bone didn't really want one, but any opportunity to inconvenience Gilbert was one worth taking.

"And you?" Gilbert asked Walker, his tone decidedly colder than their previous exchange.

"No thanks." Walker scowled.

Gilbert disappeared back up the stairs, and Bone let out a sigh of relief.

"God, he's even worse than I remember." He removed a notepad and his phone from his ancient, faded green rucksack, and waited for the first PC to arrive.

Five minutes later, a young officer appeared, carefully carrying an overfull plastic cup of liquidised tarmac that had the cheek to pass itself off as Colombian roast.

"PC Laura Dowds, sir," the officer said, placing the cup down in front of Bone. "From the DCI. I didn't make it." She looked up and smiled.

"This is DI Walker." Bone nodded to his colleague.

He then gestured to the empty chairs, and the PC sat.

After a few brief questions to help the officer relax, Bone cut to the chase. The PC went through events with the kind of detail that Bone would have expected a police officer to remember. The party had been organised by Sergeant Fiona Crawford — Garvey's commanding officer and long-term friend — to celebrate her own birthday, her fortieth. PC Dowds recalled that when she'd arrived, Garvey was already there, and aside from a very brief conversation in the loo involving rumours of job cuts across the force, she didn't remember speaking directly to her again, but did notice that she got drunk very quickly.

The second colleague, PC Bethany Ross, a thirty-eight-year-old, dyed-in-the-wool bobby, cried the moment she opened her mouth, and after a few failed attempts at extracting information between blubs, Bone gave up and told her to contact him if she thought of anything that might help the inquiry.

Bone continued, interviewing PC John Davenport next, who confirmed the exact time Garvey had left. When Bone queried his astonishing memory, Davenport explained that he'd checked the time immediately after Garvey had left because he'd been worried about his babysitter being out too late.

With two more partygoers to go, Bone took a short break and called Baxter.

"Any news?"

"Nothing, sir," Baxter replied. "How's it going over there?"

"Getting there. Anything on Meiklejohn Senior?"

"Still searching."

"Okay. Tell Mark to press Andy at the Fells to remember the exact time Meiklejohn left. It could be crucial." Bone hung up and turned to Walker. "I know Andy said Meiklejohn was pissed, but he could have been faking it. Who'd really have taken enough notice to tell the difference?"

"It's certainly possible, sir," Walker agreed.

They continued the interviews. Last up was Harvey's boss, Sergeant Fiona Crawford, primed like a coiled spring. She marched in and, stopping in front of the table, waited for Bone to invite her to sit. Once seated, she eyeballed Bone and Walker, then pushed her shaking hands into her lap.

"She's dead, isn't she?" she said before Bone could start.

"What makes you say that?"

"The Peek-a-boo case. I've been reading up on it."

"This is not the Peek-a-boo case, Sergeant Crawford," Bone replied, as Crawford continued to stare him down. "It was your birthday that night, is that correct?"

"Yes, and something I won't be celebrating again," she said, her lips tightening.

"I understand you're very good friends with PC Garvey?" Bone continued.

"Hazel looks up to me. You know she lost her parents when she was a child?"

"No, I didn't know. How did they die?"

"Car accident. Their car hit an oncoming lorry. Hazel was thrown from the vehicle and survived, but her parents were killed instantly."

"That's awful. How old was she?"

"Six, I believe."

Bone sighed. "So who took care of her?"

"Her granny. She's still alive but is now in care with dementia."

"Well, it sounds like it's good she has you." Bone attempted to keep the angry sergeant on side. "So could you tell me about that night?"

"Hazel wasn't right. I knew the minute she arrived."

"In what way?" Bone turned over a new page in his notebook and scribbled.

"She confides in me, you know, like a big sister."

"Or a mum?" Bone said.

"I'm not that old!" Crawford recoiled. "She would talk to me about anything — her life and relationships, all the personal stuff."

"Did she talk to you that night?"

"She was trying to hide it, as it was my birthday and she probably didn't want to upset me or spoil the mood, but I could see it in her face."

"See what?"

"Fear."

"Fear of what?"

"Who, more like." Crawford unlocked her clenched hands and dropped them to her sides, as though preparing to defend herself. "This is quite difficult. I don't want to get in trouble here or breach confidentiality or anything."

"Go on — it's okay. If this is important it could help find Hazel," Walker added.

"Her husband, the right honourable Chief Officer McLean." His title spilled out of Crawford's mouth like a foul- tasting poison.

"Were they having problems?" Bone pressed.

"Problems? He's the one with the problem."

"What do you mean?"

"When they first got married, things seemed great between them. Hazel would bore us to tears about how he'd spoil her with romantic dinners and posh holidays. But it didn't last long."

"What happened?"

"The romantic stories stopped, and Hazel seemed more serious, withdrawn. And then one evening, she turned up on my doorstep and she just broke down."

"Was McLean abusing her, then?"

"He didn't make her happy anymore, put it that way."

"Did he hit her?"

"She never said that, though I wouldn't be surprised. He's more of the psychological torturing type. Abuse isn't always about fists."

"What did he do to her?"

"He undermined her, treated her like shit. Her confidence was shot to hell. He was controlling her — or trying to."

"Did you ever see him behave like that with her?"

"No, but that night, she told me she'd defied him to come to my party. It was so upsetting to see her that way…just being crushed by that monstrous arsehole." She glanced up. "Sorry, I'm just so angry."

"Do you think he might have anything to do with her disappearance?"

"It would be wrong to say that, but Hazel would have wanted me to tell you about him."

"Thank you, Sergeant. You've been extremely helpful." Bone smiled.

"I don't want to be the one who points the finger at him. He's too powerful, and I need to keep my job. I have kids." A flutter of anxiety crossed her brow.

"Don't worry, Sergeant Crawford," Bone replied. "We'll keep your name out of our enquiries for now."

"Thank you, I'd appreciate that."

"But farther down the line, we may have to ask you to provide a statement."

Crawford sighed and then nodded. "If it results in justice for Hazel, then what else would she have me do?" she replied, blinking back the tears.

As Bone and Walker were heading out through the front foyer, a tall man in a sharp suit appeared from a side door and approached them.

"DCI Bone?"

"Yes?"

"I'm DS Sanjit Mohan. Could I have a quick word?"

"No problem. This is DI Walker, by the way," Bone said.

Walker nodded.

"I understand that the RCU has been called in on this and I totally respect that, but PC Garvey is our colleague from this station, and we would all like to help as much as we can to catch the bastard who did this."

"Thank you, DS Mohan, and I'm so sorry. I believe PC Garvey was an outstanding officer."

"One of the best, and a very dear colleague." DS Mohan frowned. "I've been talking with the officers who attended that night, and in my view, from what they've said about PC Garvey's condition when she left the pub, it sounds very much to me like her drink had been spiked."

"Why would you say that?" Bone asked.

"I've known Hazel for a number of years, and to be honest, she wasn't the sort of person to lose herself to alcohol. She is — sorry, *was* — very level-headed. Her behaviour that night seems out of character; it's just not quite right."

"What if she was very upset about something, could that trigger irrational behaviour in her?" Walker added.

"As I said, she wasn't the type to lose control like that. It just wasn't her, you know?"

"That is extremely useful information," Bone said.

"Like I said, I want to help, sir. We all do."

"You and your colleagues here have invaluable knowledge and understanding of PC Garvey's working life, and perhaps her world outside of the station too, that will hopefully help us unlock this investigation as quickly as possible. So let's keep the communication lines open, eh?"

"Will do." DS Mohan nodded and returned to the back room.

Back at the car, Bone called Baxter again.

"Any news on the identification of the body?"

"SOC are still on it, but I would expect they'll have a confirmed ID very soon," Baxter said. "I've found an arrest sheet for John Meiklejohn, from three months ago."

"What for?"

"He was picked up for urinating in the town gardens, but a couple of teenage girls also complained that he had exposed himself to them."

"Lovely."

"But all charges were dropped."

"Okay, thanks. Keep hunting." Bone hung up.

"Where now?" Walker asked, stepping reluctantly back into Bone's death trap time machine.

"I feel we should pay our respects to Mr Meiklejohn Senior, don't you?"

"Oh Jesus." Walker fastened her seat belt and double-checked it was secure.

THIRTEEN

John Meiklejohn's tumbledown horror story of a smallholding was located at the very end of Back Brae Lane, about three miles out of Kilwinnoch, tucked into the lower slopes of the Campsie Fells. If Hollywood was ever in need of a suitable location for the next *Texas Chainsaw Massacre* film, then Meiklejohn's place was prime real estate. Rusting skeletons of twisted scrap metal and broken glass, disembowelled car engines, and empty chassis were piled in front of a looming metal grabber that swung back and forth, threatening to plunge at any second.

"What a cesspit." Walker grimaced as Bone parked the Saab in the yard.

"Aye, it's no palace, that's for sure," he replied, eyeballing the chaos. The place unsettled him, there was an uneasiness in the air that twisted Bone's gut.

Bracing themselves, the pair stepped out and into a quagmire of mud and engine sludge.

"Not again," Walker groaned, her entire foot disappearing into a mini sinkhole. "God, I hate my job."

Meiklejohn's rotting rubble of a but and ben lay directly ahead, the windows boarded or taped up with bin bags, half the roof tiles missing, and a small oak tree sprouting from one of the lopsided chimney pots. Bone pointed at the acrid beige smoke pluming from the top and leaking from gaping holes in its side.

"Looks like somebody's in."

Together, they staggered and splodged their way to a panel of bitumen-smeared plywood propped up against a gaping hole in the stone where the door was meant to be. Bone rapped the panel, and it rolled sideways. Walker caught it just in time, and it stopped. When there was no reply from inside, Bone thumped the wood again.

"Who is it?" a rasping voice called out from whatever repugnant horrors awaited them beyond.

"DCI Bone, John. May we come in?"

"No!" Meiklejohn retorted.

Bone slid the board sideways, unglued his hands from the sticky surface, and pushed his way in, with Walker following reluctantly behind. The first thing that hit him was a sickly sweet smell of rotting meat. The space in front was almost pitch-black, and it took him a few seconds to adjust to the sudden loss of light.

Meiklejohn slouched at the far side of the room, hunkered down by a small gas lamp. Bone was shocked. The man had lost all his hair since he'd last encountered him and looked incredibly gaunt, like some nightmarish Hitchcockian apparition. Bizarrely, he was also wearing what looked like a 60s-style housecoat.

"What's with the smell, John?" Bone asked, almost ready to arrest him right there on the spot.

"What smell?"

"Like someone's died," Walker added.

"Oh aye. It's my poor dug." He turned and pointed at something in the far corner. "He just keeled over."

Bone squinted into the gloom. A dark mound lay on the floor by the wall.

"Check it out," he whispered to Walker.

"Me?" She recoiled.

She reluctantly ventured towards the unidentified lump.

"Do you not have mains power anymore?" Bone stumbled over another unidentified object on the floor.

"The bastards cut me aff."

Over in the darkness, Walker let out a loud groan, and she returned, holding her hand over her nose and mouth.

"Dug right enough — half Labrador, half maggots."

"Do you not think your dog needs burying, John?" Bone ventured closer.

Meiklejohn ripped up a newspaper into strips and twisted the bundles into tight tapers.

The old man paused for a second. "I'm no buryin' nothin'," he said defiantly.

"Well, I'm sure your dog would prefer the dignity of a decent funeral than ending up a feast for the bluebottles." Bone closed in farther and leant on the table within a few inches of Meiklejohn, scrutinising his filthy, pockmarked features. "I have to say, you're not the fine specimen of a fella I knew back when your son was off murdering people," he observed.

Meiklejohn slammed his fists down on the table. "Have you come to harass me? Is that how you get your kicks, frightenin' auld men?"

"Oh — I think we both know that's not true. You'd scare Freddie Krueger into an early grave, John," Walker waded in.

"How's things been then? Have you been up to anything exciting?" Bone smiled.

"Get fucked."

"That's not very nice, John. Not very nice at all."

Meiklejohn continued to stare ahead, refusing to make eye contact.

"Where were you on Tuesday night?"

"No comment."

Bone laughed. "This isn't a formal interrogation. Just two mates shooting the breeze." He asked again. "Well?"

"Here," Meiklejohn replied eventually. "Like always."

"And can anyone vouch for your whereabouts, apart from Last Rights Lassie over there?"

"Nope."

"Well, that's all then. Thanks for your time."

Meiklejohn looked up at Bone in surprise. Then it was Bone's turn to slam his fist on the table. He leaned right in to within a Glasgow handshake of Meiklejohn's face.

"It was quite a commotion," Bone whispered in the man's grime-blackened lughole.

Meiklejohn turned his head slightly. "Whit was?"

"When my colleague here stepped out for a moment and you lunged at me."

"I've no been near you."

"And I have to say, for a sixty-nine-year-old, you put up quite a fight. But, you know, attempted assault of a police officer — well, that's bad news, isn't it, Detective Walker?"

"Oh yes, and with your criminal record, John. Ooft, five years at least, I'd say."

"This is no right. I'm reportin' you for harassment."

"No, I'll be reporting you, John." Bone leaned in closer still. "To the procurator fiscal."

Meiklejohn pulled back and held up his hands. "Aw right! What do you want?"

"Tuesday night, John. Try again."

Meiklejohn straightened up and returned to his strip tearing, but this time his hands shook. "I walked down to the Fells for a pint."

"See? That wasn't too difficult, was it? What time was that?"

"I don't know. I don't have a watch or a clock. It was getting dark."

"Dusk?"

"Aye. I walked over. I had a couple and walked back."

"Who was on the bar that night?"

"I can't remember. Maybe the big lad."

"Andy Coates?" Bone asked. He glanced back at Walker, but she'd disappeared.

"Aye."

"Who else was there? Did you speak to anyone?"

"Nobody speaks to me."

Bone tapped the table with his knuckle.

"I had a few words with Dobson," Meiklejohn said.

"A few words?"

"He said I owed him money, and I told him where to shove it."

"Did you have a barney, then?"

"With Davie Dobson? Are you havin' a laugh? I just left before it got messy."

"Anyone else?"

"Naw."

Bone kicked the table, and Meiklejohn jumped back in surprise.

"Sure?" Bone demanded.

"Nobody else. Just Dobson."

"So when did you leave?"

"I dunno. Two pints after."

"Andy threw you out, didn't he?"

"I just left."

"Where did you go after the Fells?"

"I told you. I went home. Naw—" He stopped suddenly, as though remembering something. "I had a poke of chips."

"Where?"

"The chippie, where else? I was starvin'."

"And then you went home?"

"Well, I'm here so I must have." Meiklejohn sneered.

"Sir?" Walker called out.

Bone turned but couldn't see her. "Where are you?"

"Through here."

Bone negotiated the carcass and carnage to the back of the room. Meiklejohn had stopped tearing and had instead turned to look.

"Where?" Bone called out again.

"This way," Walker repeated.

Bone spotted a narrow wooden door and pushed it with his fist. Inside, it was pitch-dark, but Walker flashed her phone torch light back and forth across the walls and floor to help him locate her. Bone caught a glimpse of a mattress in the centre of the room and a few bottles and cans strewn across a stone floor.

"Check this out," Walker said, directing the beam to the back wall.

The light illuminated a makeshift gallery of images and newspaper cuttings, crudely taped to the flaking plaster. Snapshots of Robert Meiklejohn's chilling police mugshot, press release images of the victims, headlines and articles, and then — finally — the light settled on an image of the scene of the explosion, and an old photo of Bone, from when he was a uniformed officer. Walker quickly redirected the torch to the floor.

"Sorry, sir," she said.

Bone shook his head and stomped back to Meiklejohn, avoiding the mess. Walker gingerly picked her way through the debris after him.

"That's quite an art display you've got in there," Bone snapped at the old man.

"My business. I'm not breaking any laws."

"Apart from the laws of decency, or respect for your son's victims, maybe," Walker said.

"My son's dead. I'm his faither."

"Yes, you are, and I can't begin to imagine how he became the monster he was, can you, DI Walker?"

"Beats me." Walker shrugged.

"Has there been another murder or something?" Meiklejohn asked.

Bone leaned in again, and Meiklejohn pulled back.

"Now that's interesting, John. And why would you say that?"

"Well, you're back here harassin' me again, aren't you?"

"Good point, smart arse." Bone grinned. He straightened up. "We'll be away now for a wee bit of late lunch at the chippie, but don't worry, we'll be back again very soon, I'm sure."

As they left, Bone stopped at the entrance. "And bury your bloody dog."

FOURTEEN

Sandino's chip shop and ice cream parlour was a legend in Kilwinnoch, and the town's average BMI was testament to the chippie's popularity. The Sandino family had been a central fixture for over eighty years, since the first wave of Italian immigrants landed in the 1930s and 40s and changed Scottish culture forever. Signor Carlo Sandino — the third proprietor of the eatery and the great-grandson of its founder, Paulo Sandino — was a jovial, well-loved character, always inclined to chat rather than sell any food. The place had a fine reputation for culinary innovation; Carlo's grandfather introduced the town to spaghetti fritters, and the family's fame was sealed when Carlo, following in his grandfather's footsteps, added a deep-fried bridie to the menu —a particularly popular choice with punters on late Saturday nights.

Bone dropped Walker outside, where a queue was already forming for the chippie's first serve of the day. Mr Sandino was at the fryer in his white short-sleeved chef's shirt, with the collar buttoned to the top, old school.

116

Walker pushed her way through the line of ravenous pensioners and into the shop. Mr Sandino was busy dropping a hefty pail of chipped spuds into bubbling fat, which hissed and spat, engulfing the shop in a nuclear-sized plume of smoke. The diminutive owner glanced up mid-alchemy.

"Ten minutes until we open." He wiped spatters of hot fat from his burn-scarred arms. Then he looked up again. "Miss Walker!" he cried with near-operatic aplomb. "Bella signora degli altipiani!" his aria continued. "How are you?"

"Good afternoon. I'm okay, thanks," Walker shouted over the deafening hiss of boiling fat.

"And how are your parents? They still on that beautiful island? He stirred the fryer vigorously.

"My mum passed away in September."

"So sorry to hear. It was the cancer, yes?" Mr Sandino said, his melodious Italian accent battling bravely with broad Glaswegian brogue. "Must be tough for your father."

"He's in Oban now. The farm on Lewis was getting too much for him."

"This is good. He needs to be with some company now, but it's so tough, eh?"

Walker nodded.

"Chips will be ready in under ten minutes, Miss Walker." He gave the fryer another hefty stir. "This bloody half-price lunch offer will be the death of me." He pointed at the never-ending queue outside.

"It's a police matter," Walker continued.

"Oh?" Sandino paused his stirring. "How can I help you?"

"I'll let you deal with those chips first, no problem," Walker said. "Can't upset that lot out there, eh?"

Mr Sandino, now sweating profusely as he battled with the fryer, gave the chips a couple more stirs and stopped. "Okay, we let that work its magic now," he said with an assured grin.

"They do smell good, though." Walker 's stomach rumbled.

"You can have the first poke out of the fryer, on the house."

There was a thump at the door, and then an over-eager elderly man stuck his head in.

"Five more minutes, Mr Robertson," Mr Sandino bellowed.

The pensioner retreated to the front of the queue as the chef shook his head. "Jesus Christ. Every day it's the same."

"You've created a town full of addicts." Walker laughed.

"Aye, so what is this police matter?" He opened the side hatch and joined her on the shop floor.

"Was John Meiklejohn in your shop last Tuesday night, possibly around eleven-thirty p.m.?" Walker looked down at the man, surprised by how small Mr Sandino was up close.

"Last Tuesday, you say?" He scratched at the fat burns on his arms.

"Twenty-eighth of September," Walker added.

"Ah, now Marco would have been on that night. I play La Scopa."

Walker shook her head.

"The cards, you know, Italian style. I play at the bowling club with my friends. We bet a little, but I shouldn't tell you that, eh?" He laughed.

"Is Marco here?"

"He's out the back at the freezer, or he was the last time I checked him up, but he's probably back in that bloody yard on his bloody phone." He returned behind the counter and gave the fryer a quick stir on the way past.

He disappeared through the rear door and hollered at his son. They both emerged, and Marco, who was around sixteen years old, gave his dad double 'V's behind his back.

"Like I said — on his bloody phone."

Mr Sandino turned and ranted at his son in Italian, Walker picking out only one word she recognised: 'idiota'.

"Hi, Marco," Walker said with a smile.

"Aye," Marco mumbled.

"I'm Detective Inspector Walker. I need to ask you a couple of questions, okay?"

Marco shrugged.

"Answer the inspector, Marco," Mr Sandino elbowed his son.

"Your dad says you were working here last Tuesday night, is that correct?"

"Aye, that's right. Have I done something wrong?" Marco replied with not the slightest hint of an Italian accent.

"No, not at all. I just need you to confirm something for me."

"Aw right. Aye, no bother."

"Can you remember if John Meiklejohn came in and bought a bag of chips, maybe around eleven-thirty p.m.?"

"Who?"

"John Meiklejohn, the father of Robert Meiklejohn."

"The Peek-a-boo pazzo," Mr Sandino said to his son.

"I'm no sure." Marco scratched the top of his head.

"He might have been really drunk?" Walker added.

"Everybody's always really drunk," the son joked. "It was busy. It's always busy, and I'm always flat out. I don't have time to—" He stopped and glanced over at his dad.

"Workshy, that's his problem," Mr Sandino moaned. "Some generation, this. They have no idea. His grandfather worked eighteen-hour shifts running this place. All he does is go on his phone with the girls."

"Dad!" Marco's baby-faced cheeks glowed a deep shade of crimson.

Mr Sandino suddenly spun round, clearly remembering the lunch rush. "Fanculo!" he yelled. Grabbing a basket, he scooped the newly cooked chips out of the fryer and transferred them to the serving bin. "Excuse, but I have to open now. Marco!"

Marco went over to help his dad excavate the chips from the oil. He stopped and turned back to Walker.

"Is he a down-and-out? I mean, does he look like one?" he asked.

"You'd know if you'd seen him," Walker replied. "He's permanently filthy, like the dirt's tattooed on his skin. He's a skeleton on a diet, and he wears any kind of clothes he can dig out of waste heaps or pilfer from washing lines."

"I remember him now. He's the guy who didn't have enough money for the chips and went total when I said he couldn't have them. In the end I just gave in to get rid of him so I could close up."

"Are you sure it was him?"

"Deffo. He was really weird n'aw. There were two women in the queue, and he was sayin' stuff to them."

"What like?"

"Ach, ye know, mingin' stuff. They told him to fuck off."

"Marco!" Mr Sandino shouted. "What have I told you?"

"Just quoting the exact words, Dad." Marco huffed.

"And what time was this?" Walker pressed.

"About half eleven. That's when we normally close, but probably a wee bit earlier. Twenty past maybe?"

He squinted at his dad, and Mr Sandino shook his head.

"That's really helpful, Marco. Thank you. And do you have any security cameras in here that might have captured Meiklejohn in the shop that night?"

"Dad?"

"Yes, up there." Mr Sandino pointed at a tiny lens in the corner. "But it automatically deletes after two or three days, so it might be gone."

"If you could check when you're not busy, that would be great. Just give me a shout at the station when you know."

Mr Sandino nodded. "Okay, Marco. Go get half a dozen bridies and some fillets from the fridge, and maybe a few haggis and sausage." He shovelled more chips into the server. "I'll let the starving millions in."

"Thank you, Mr Sandino," Walker said.

"It's wonderful to see you, Miss Walker." Mr Sandino joined her at the door. "And please say hello to your father from us, and tell him if he ever comes to Kilwinnoch, there is a bridie supper waiting for him here."

"I will, Mr Sandino, thanks. He'd love your speciality."

"I hope your investigation goes good, and I'll have a look for the video."

He opened the door, and Mr Robertson pushed past.

"Aboot bloody time, it's perishin' oot there, Carlo." He was followed by a stampede of voracious octogenarians, more excited than a gaggle of teenage girls at a Beatles gig.

"Don't forget this." Mr Sandino handed Walker a bag of steaming-hot chips, and he fought his way back to the counter.

"Right, who's first?" Mr Sandino called out, deliberately avoiding eye contact with Mr Robertson who had spread his elbows wide on the counter to secure pole position.

"I'm bloody first!" Mr Robertson barked back.

"Haha, every time." Mr Sandino beamed warmly at his most loyal but belligerent customer.

FIFTEEN

"Present for you," Walker said, dropping the still-warm bag of chips onto Mullens' desk. On her short walk to the station, she had fought valiantly to avoid temptation and had consumed only three, a personal best.

Mullens instantly stopped what he was doing. "Is that what I think it is?" He slowly peeled open the grease-stained bag and sniffed. "Oh, dear God. I love you. Will you marry me?"

"Inconceivable on so many levels," Walker scoffed. "Where's the DCI?"

"Here." Bone's head popped up from beneath the coffee machine. "Just searching for a new packet of Columbian. Anyone buy some recently?"

Silence.

"Miserable bastards doesn't even come close."

"I'll go and get some," Harper offered.

"You're okay. I just could do with a quick fix before I brave the morgue." Bone straightened up. "But cold turkey it will have to be."

"Would you like me to come with you, sir?" Walker asked.

"No, it's fine. How did you get on at Sandino's?"

"Spectacularly well," Mullens mumbled through a mouthful of rapidly congealing fat.

"Carlo's boy was on last Tuesday night. He confirmed Meiklejohn had been in at approx. eleven-twenty," Walker said.

"Bugger. But let's see what the man in black says. Serial Killer Senior is not coming off the incident board just yet."

Walker glanced up at the whiteboard, now filling up with names, notes, bullet headers, and arrows crisscrossing this way and that. When she turned back, Bone had already gone.

The morgue was located in the basement of the town's cottage hospital. Though small, it was normally adequate for most post-mortems. When Bone arrived, Cash was waiting for him by the door of the PM room.

"Wear these," he said, handing Bone a mask, rubber gloves, and another pair of delightful overshoes.

After an intimate war with an assortment of elastic straps, Bone followed Cash inside.

PC Garvey's covered body was laid out on the examination table, the sterile white plastic shroud illuminated under a bright LED spotlight. Bone flinched. It was the worst part of his job, and even after nearly twenty years of policing, it could still slither right under his skin.

"So, there she lies," Cash said as he peeled back the cover.

Bone took a sharp breath.

"The cause of death is most likely skull fracture and brain injury from multiple impact of soil and rocks." Cash tilted the head slightly to the left, revealing a large open wound in the scalp. "The victim also has three broken ribs, possibly sustained when the hole was filled, but the bruising is more consistent with a fall or a push, perhaps by her assailant."

"What about time of death?"

"A little trickier, as always. But the discolouration around the abdomen here is indicative of early stage putrification."

Bone swallowed hard.

"Are you okay?" Cash asked.

"Fine, go on."

"So, she's been in the ground for at least six days."

"So a short time between her absence being reported and her death, then?"

"I would say so, yes. We ran a battery of tests on the deceased's blood and we've found significant traces of gamma hydroxybutyrate acid." He glanced up. "GHB."

"Date rape drug?"

"That's what the tabloids call it, but there's no sign of sexual assault. Also, alcohol, as we would expect, and diazepam."

"To knock her out completely?"

"Or maybe she had her own prescription for anxiety or a sleep disorder?"

Cash gently picked up Garvey's left hand, the tie marks still visible on the wrist, and he straightened her fingers.

"We found something else. See this?" he said and isolated the index finger, twisting the nail upwards.

Bone leaned in closer. There was still some residual dirt clinging to the nails, with hints of a lilac varnish all but obliterated.

"We extracted a few nylon fibres from under this broken nail. Perhaps from the assailant, or from a carpet or furniture, or even car upholstery when she was transported to the crime scene."

"Or from her own home?"

"Yes, there is that, too. We're running a match on them and hopefully we should have results in the next few hours." Cash pushed Garvey's limp arm back onto the slab. "So there you have it." He shook his head. "Life is so precious, so desperately fragile, isn't it? One minute we're here and the next we're gone."

Oh God, here we go, Bone thought, anticipating another one of Cash's infamous existential rants.

"And in a few years, no one will even remember us," Cash continued, pulling the sheet over Garvey's body. "So many lives passing through, just snuffed out and gone." He stood motionless for a moment, staring at the plastic shroud. "The futility of existence."

"Are you sure you're in the right job, Andrew?" Bone smiled.

"My work serves to remind me that we'd better just get on with it, or it'll be over before it's even begun—"

"Right, okay, thanks, Andrew," Bone interrupted. "I'd better be away then and make the most of the little time I've left."

Cash walked Bone to the door.

"I'm sorry Duncan. This must be tough after the Peek-a-boo case."

"I've had better days," Bone admitted.

"I'll get those results to you asap." Cash held the door open.

Bone nodded politely, but as soon as Cash had disappeared back inside, he ran upstairs and into the nearest loo. Stumbling into a cubicle, he slammed it shut and locked the door. PC Garvey's broken body on the slab had brought back some of the darkest memories of the Peek-a-boo case that he'd spent months trying to eliminate from his mind; grotesque images of dying and dead police officers, grieving and angry loved ones screaming in his face, and Meiklejohn's sneering grin seconds before the pipe bomb had exploded.

He fumbled in his suit pocket for his handkerchief and held it up to his face and mouth. He took five or six short, panic-induced breaths, and slowly counted backwards from twenty, a technique he'd learnt in counselling. Another two or three, and his heart slowed, his breaths deepened. He continued to count twelve…eleven…ten. Gradually, his breathing settled. He wiped the sweat from his brow with the handkerchief, unlocked the door, and staggered to the sink. He turned on the cold tap and splashed water on his face to try to recover himself and calm the roar in his head. Glancing up at his gaunt, harrowed expression, he spotted a hooded figure standing directly behind him. It lifted its head, partially exposing a now familiar charred cheekbone and an empty eye socket.

"My old friend," the creature hissed.

Bone spun round in horror, but instead of the apparition, the startled CFO was hovering in front of him.

"Are you okay?" Cash ventured towards Bone.

Bone stood half paralysed as the real world slammed back into his brain, like a car smashing into a wall. He leaned back on the sink and rubbed unconsciously at his scar.

"Yes," Bone mumbled. "I get this from time to time. It's nothing. Just a side effect from the operation," he lied, and it was clear from Cash's expression that he thought it was a lie, too.

"This whole copycat thing is the worst nightmare for any detective, but for you it's like revisiting hell."

"I'm okay. It's important we catch this animal before we lose another cop."

"But your health is important, too."

"I'm fine, really," Bone said, and with an attempt at a reassuring nod, he left the loo.

With luck, Cash won't report this up the food chain, he thought and headed up to the living air and the outside world.

SIXTEEN

A dvocate McLean's grandiose house was located in Horsewalk Avenue, probably the only street in Kilwinnoch that could be classified as posh. For those in the town with ambition — and they were few and far between — it was where they aspired to be. As for the rest of the rabble, they looked upon the residents of this tree-lined, semi-detached paradise with either genuine contempt or as an Aladdin's cave of potential knockoffs. As Bone and Walker approached the imposing Edwardian red-brick pile, two uniforms by the front gate eyed him up.

"DCI Bone and DI Walker." They flashed their lanyards.

One uniform nodded.

"Is he in?" Bone asked.

"Aye, but he's no seeing anyone," Uniform One said, kicking the toe of his Doc into the tarmac.

The other straightened the radio clinging precariously from his yellow jacket.

"Okay," Bone replied. He carried on through the gate and up the drive to the house.

A third uniform loitered by the immaculately painted oak front door.

"DCI Bone," Bone said to the officer.

"Hello, sir, ma'am. I'm PC Willits, one of the assigned liaison officers. Mr McLean is refusing our help."

"I know. Bill and Ben at the gate told me."

Willits tried to conceal a smile.

"Are you alone?" Bone asked.

"No, my colleague is round at the back door."

"So how long has he been alone in there?"

"A few hours, sir, maybe two. I'm not sure."

"And he's definitely in there?"

"He hasn't left his property."

"And alive? I mean — he hasn't done anything daft?"

"Oh, I didn't think…"

"Bloody hell." Bone shook his head in dismay and rapped the heavy brass knocker against the solid panel. After a moment, he thumped again, and then a third time, each blow more forceful than the last. No reply. Kneeling, he pushed at the ornate brass letterbox and peered inside. An impressively spacious hallway led to a grand mahogany staircase that coiled its way up to the first floor. But there was no sign of McLean.

Squeezing his face up to the letterbox, Bone hollered through the aperture, "Mr McLean, it's Detective Chief Inspector Duncan Bone!"

Bone paused and listened. Noises filtered through from somewhere on the far side of the house. Then

131

came a loud crash, followed by incoherent shouting. Bone tried again.

"Mr McLean, it's the police, open up!" Bone thought he'd escalate authority levels but suspected it wouldn't make the slightest difference. "Can we get in round the back?" he asked the liaison officer.

"Aye, sir, this way."

The detectives followed the uniform round the side of the house, up a side path, and then negotiating the bins, they squeezed through a narrow gate in a high brick wall with broken glass concreted in along the top.

"Does the property have a security system, CCTV, that sort of thing?" Bone asked the liaison as they worked their way around the side of a greenhouse.

"I'm not sure, sir. You'd have to ask Bill and — er — the two officers at the gate. They might know."

Once past the greenhouse, they found themselves in a substantial and beautifully kept rear garden with trimmed borders, a large, manicured lawn, and a pond impersonating an inland loch.

"We definitely picked the wrong career," Walker said.

When they reached the rear corner of a modernist glass extension, Bone peered through one of the towering bifold doors that stretched across the full height and width of the back wall.

"There he is," Willits said.

"Where?" Bone and Walker asked in unison, their faces pressed up to the glass.

"Through that door at the back of the kitchen." Willits tapped the pane with her finger.

"Oh yes," Bone said.

McLean, was propped up at a desk, his head in his hands and leaning forward.

Bone rattled the pane with his knuckle. McLean ignored him. He thumped the glass again, this time with more force. McLean glanced up for a moment, his face devoid of expression.

"It's DCI Bone," the detective mouthed.

McLean finally got up.

A moment later, a door on the side of the extension slowly opened.

"Mr McLean," Bone said.

McLean marched back into the house. Halfway across the kitchen, he stopped.

"Well?" he exclaimed. "Are you coming?"

"Wait here for now," Bone said to the liaison officer. "I'll call you if I need you."

He gestured to Walker, and they followed McLean in.

"Before you launch into your 'we are so sorry to inform you' speech," McLean said, returning to his desk at the rear of a substantial home office, "I know that my wife has been found, and to be honest, I was never expecting any other outcome." He sifted through papers strewn across the desktop.

"We are so sorry for your loss," Bone said, despite McLean's warning. "We hoped that—"

"Hope?" McLean barked back.

Bone noticed a half-empty bottle of Macallan sitting on the desk.

"All we can hope is that she died instantly and didn't suffer," McLean said.

"We believe that is probably the case, sir," Bone replied.

"This is all so difficult." McLean's movements were becoming more frantic. He suddenly stopped. "Who is this woman?" He pointed accusingly at Walker.

"DI Walker, sir. We met briefly the other day." She fixed her eyes on him.

"I thought you were one of those bloody family liaison officers. Lord preserve me from their vacuous platitudes." He stopped. "You were on the Meiklejohn case with him, weren't you?" he asked, his accusatory tone continuing to escalate.

"Yes, sir."

"Good, so you will know how your boss completely fucked up the prosecution." He picked up the bottle and poured a large double into a chunky crystal glass.

"The suspect booby-trapped his flat, sir," Walker returned. "And DCI Bone was nearly killed in the blast."

"And now back at work." McLean took a large swig of whisky. "Right as rain and fit for duty."

"Yes, sir," Walker replied angrily and glanced over at her boss.

"And now we have a martyr, inspiring fanatics to follow in his footsteps. Is that how you read it, Inspector Bone?"

"Our investigations are ongoing, sir, and we will, of course, keep you informed of any developments." Bone replied, refusing to rise to the bait.

McLean finished his whisky and poured another glass.

"Are you sure you should be...?" Bone said.

"What, drinking?" McLean sneered. "You expect me to deal with the murder of my wife sober?" He guzzled another mouthful. "Aside from coming to inform me of your continuing incompetence, is there anything else I can help you with? As you can see, I am extremely busy and I need to go through my briefs before court tomorrow."

"I'm not sure you should be working, sir," Bone said.

McLean let out a loud, cynical laugh. "That's rich."

"I'm afraid you may be asked to confirm your wife's identity at the cottage hospital."

"Yes, I do know that, DCI Bone. I am the chief prosecutor. I know how it works." He raised his glass, then slammed it down on his desk. "Is that everything? I'd rather you left now."

"Sorry for your—" Bone started again.

"Save it." McLean raised his hand. The detectives turned to leave but Bone stopped.

"Just one other question," he said.

McLean sighed and rested his hands impatiently on the desk.

"On the night of your wife's disappearance…"

"And brutal and avoidable murder, Inspector," McLean snapped back.

"Did you have an argument?" Bone persevered.

"What?" McLean winced.

"Did you have words with each other? Perhaps you were angry about her going out?"

"What is this?"

"We're just trying to piece together your wife's state of mind that night — if she was upset, it might have affected her behaviour."

"We don't row, Inspector," McLean fired back.

"All couples row, it's part of a healthy relationship, isn't it?" Walker cut in.

"We *never* argued. I don't know where you are going with this but I'm becoming increasingly irritated with your presence in my house and the fact that you are on this case. Please leave right now, Inspector, and take your—" he paused to reconsider his words "—colleague with you."

"It has come to light that your wife had a heart-to-heart with a close friend in the pub that night," Bone persisted.

"Who?"

"We are trying to establish facts, sir. The close friend said your wife described her relationship with you as—" He turned to Walker, who flicked open her notepad theatrically, and after a quick scan, she said "—Toxic."

"I've had enough of this!" McLean said, jumping to his feet.

"She went on to describe how you had attempted to forbid her from attending the birthday party and that you systematically undermined, bullied, and controlled her."

"I would like you to leave *now!*" McLean raged.

"Would you consider yourself to be an abusive husband, Mr McLean?"

"If you don't leave this instance, I'll call your boss and have you physically removed from my property," McLean snarled. He marched to his office door, his whole body shaking with rage, or perhaps fear. "You have just lost any hope of saving your job, DCI Bone. Goodbye."

He held the door and the detectives left.

Back in the garden, Walker pushed her fists into her coat pocket. "I thought I was going to lamp him one."

"Yup, a top-drawer dickhead."

"Are you sure it was a good idea to pick a fight with him, though? I mean, he's a pretty formidable enemy."

"I want him to know that we know who he is. If he's involved in PC Garvey's murder, his fury with me might just make him fall over his own lies."

"And if not?"

"Even if he had nothing to do with it, our sanctimonious, wife-abusing pillar of the community deserves everything that's coming to him."

"I just hope we're still in the force to see it through," Walker said.

"Bullies come a cropper in the end — they always do," Bone replied, and headed for the gate.

SEVENTEEN

After another long and exhausting shift, Bone couldn't face returning to his empty flat. Instead he detoured to the Kinloch Hotel, a bland, corporate three-star situated inconveniently on the farthest edge of town and close enough to the sewage works to add to its fragrant appeal. Designed for business travellers and lost tourists, it was therefore usually deserted and an ideal hideaway for Bone to enjoy a quiet drink undisturbed.

The barman looked up from his glass polishing with surprise when Bone entered the desolate lounge.

"Good evening, sir," the over-groomed and heavily perfumed young man said enthusiastically but with an air of desperation.

"80 shilling…" Bone leaned on the counter to read the barman's lurid yellow name badge. "Zak."

"Er — sorry, sir, the 80 is off."

"Guinness?"

"That's off, too."

"Jesus," Bone muttered. "Did you have a mad rush earlier — a football coach or something?"

"Ach no, sir, it's just it goes off 'cos nobody's drinking it."

"Not the best of adverts for your bar," Bone commented.

"No — aye — ha!" Zak chuckled nervously. "We do have Tennent's and this new pale ale from…" He stuck his head over the counter to read the pump badge, and a waft of aftershave hit Bone square in the face. "Estonia, I think. To be honest, you're the first customer in since lunchtime, and that was a builder who only came in to use the loo. It's total pish, but they're payin' me to clean these clean glasses, so I'm no bothered," he replied, his faux South Side accent peeling away.

"Tennent's will be fine," Bone said.

"You sit down and I'll bring it over."

"Wow, spoilt," Bone scoffed. "Don't pull a tendon on the way over."

Zak laughed and turned to pick out a clean glass from the vast array of choices lined up behind him. Hesitating for a moment on which empty chair to choose, Bone plumped for one by the coal-effect fire.

"There you go," Zak said moments later.

"That was quick."

"Aye, I'm totally wasted here." He squinted at Bone again. "You're a copper, right?"

"Correct. Is it that obvious?"

"No, I recognise you. Inspector Bone?"

"Correct again. Have you thought about joining the force?" Bone joked.

"Aye — no — ha!" Zak chortled again. "You're the Peek-a-boo guy, aren't you?"

"It's not exactly how I define myself," Bone returned.

"I bet you can't believe it."

"What?"

"That nutter on the loose again."

"What are you talking about?"

"You must have heard about it, surely?" Zak pulled a face that made him look even younger.

"Heard what?" The barman's enthusiasm was beginning to irritate Bone.

"Hold on." He dashed behind the counter and returned with a newspaper. "Here."

Bone snatched it out of his hand and unfolded it. The front page screamed back at him:

Peek-a-boo Kills Again

The sub-heading was as subtle as a sewage drain:

Brain-damaged Cop Leads Hunt for Psychopath

Underneath was a picture of Bone at one of the first press conferences and a second of him being unceremoniously stretchered out of Robert Meiklejohn's bomb-destroyed flat.

"Fuck!" he roared and threw the paper down on the table.

"Everything all right?" Zak asked in alarm.

Bone slapped a tenner on the bar and stormed out.

"What about your change?" Zak called back.

But Bone had already gone.

EIGHTEEN

Records officer, Sam Tozier, checked his watch: 9:48 p.m. He dropped his fishing gear in the hall and went upstairs. "That's me off to the loch," he said to his wife, poking his head round the bedroom door, but Carol, a long-suffering fishing widow, or so she would believe, was already asleep, her hands still clinging to her bedtime read. He leaned over and eased the book from her grip, removed the cushions propped up behind her, and watched as she slowly settled back into a deep sleep. He switched off the light and crept out.

At the car, he bundled his fishing tackle into the boot and climbed in behind the wheel. Setting a canvas bag down on the passenger seat, he opened the straps and quickly scanned the contents. He glanced in the rearview mirror and with a shaking finger wiped a dried crust of saliva from the corner of his mouth, careful to avoid eye contact with himself. The shame in his eyes was too much to bear. He started up and set off in the direction of Braebank Loch.

When he reached the lochside turning, he checked the time again: 10:12. *Shit*. He put his foot down harder on the gas and carried on into the hills ahead.

Approaching Foresthills car park, about three miles farther into the Campsies, he slowed. And when he was sure it was empty, he pulled in and drove to the farthest edge of the perimeter fence. He turned off the engine and his lights, and the car park plunged into darkness.

His breathing quickened as the fear intensified. From his canvas bag he removed a box file and then stepped out of the vehicle. Fumbling with his phone, he turned on the torch and inched his way across the car park, the beam flittering back and forth haphazardly in his jittering fist. When he reached the opposite boundary, he flicked the phone until the beam landed on a weather-battered wooden shelter tucked in by a line of high conifers. He shuffled over, stepped in, and slotted the box file under the wooden bench at the back.

Returning to the car park, he spun round, his torchlight bobbing and bouncing in the dark. "I've done what you wanted," he called out, the wind stealing his voice.

He turned again, probing the light into the farthest corners, and then back up to the entrance. But there was nobody there. For a second he thought about retrieving the documents and facing the music, but then he jumped back in his car and started the engine. A flutter of movement in his rearview mirror caught his eye. He was about to turn round when something yanked his head back with force against the rest.

Instinctively, he threw a fist upwards in defence but only managed to punch himself in the cheek. Something was round his neck, pressing into his windpipe, choking him. He kicked out against the pedals to gain some leverage, but the car's engine screamed, and the grip on his throat tightened. A needle-sharp burning pain shot into his neck and he glimpsed a syringe in the assailant's gloved fist. He choked a muted *help*, but his lungs were on fire. The gloved hand shifted slightly, allowing him to gasp a mouthful of air, but the supply was short-lived. Something rough was rammed against his face, and his nose and mouth filled with a noxious, sickly-sweet stench. His eyes blurred, and in a matter of moments he was unconscious.

NINETEEN

The following morning, Bone stormed into the incident room, still raging from his previous night's read.

"Who's the big mouth, then?" he hollered at the team.

They all turned in surprise.

"Have you seen the headlines?" he continued.

"Shocking pile of shite." Mullens was first into the fray. "It certainly wasn't me. I wouldn't pee on any of them, even if their balls were on fire."

The rest of the team shook their heads and shrugged.

"No one in here has said a word, sir," Walker said, attempting to calm the situation.

"It's that weasel, McKinnon. Someone is feeding him information, and then the whole barrel of rats pick it up," Bone snarled.

"Well, it's not coming from here. We all have each other's backs — and yours, sir," Walker insisted.

Bone calmed down. "We need to keep it that way."

"I think you may have to speak to them again to keep them at bay for a bit longer," Walker added. "I'll do it if you like."

"Not yet. We've got work to do this morning. I'll speak to them later." He retreated to the coffee machine.

Walker followed.

"Are you okay?" she asked.

"As if it wasn't hard enough picking a fight with the country's leading prosecutor." He attempted a smile. "Thanks for the offer. But they need to hear it from me."

He went over to the incident board and examined the evidence trail so far: a gruesome gallery of previous victims, PC Garvey's smashed body, miserable mugshots of Meiklejohn Senior, Chief Officer McLean, and at the very top of the pyramid, Peek-a-boo himself, peering down with smug indignation. Bone ran his finger up and down his scar, pondering the pathways and connections for a few moments, and then turned back to the room.

"Will, have those files appeared yet?"

"I'm still waiting to hear back from records, sir," Harper replied. "They were still hunting for them the last time I checked."

"The whole lot is missing?"

"Apparently, yes."

"It just gets better and better," Bone exclaimed. He stormed out the door.

Down in the basement, Bone approached the records clerk, who was busy on his phone. He waited a few seconds, then lost his patience.

"Excuse me," he said briskly.

The clerk held up his hand and continued his chat. Bone slammed his palm down on the desk. The clerk looked up in surprise.

"Now that I have your attention," he growled. "Phone down — now!"

The clerk quickly said his goodbyes and hung up. "Yes?" he said to Bone, peering over his bifocals.

"DCI Bone. Where's Sam Tozier?"

"Oh, sorry, sir," the clerk said sheepishly. "Mr Tozier has been off sick for a couple of days. I've been sent over from Denny to cover for him." He pushed his phone under a pile of papers on the desk. "What can I do for you?"

"My colleague was down earlier asking about the Meiklejohn folder. Have you found it yet?"

The clerk fidgeted with the stationery on the desk. "Sorry, sir, I haven't, no."

Bone sighed. "Where's the sign-out book?"

"Yes, it's er…" The clerk rummaged around the desk, searching under his copy of *Good Homes*, but he couldn't find the book. He paused for a second, clearly thinking.

Bone shuffled his feet. "In your own time." He sighed.

"Ah yes," the clerk said with a smile of relief, and he shot down under the desk, as though he'd fallen into the hole he was digging for himself. Moments later, he re-emerged with the buried treasure. "Bingo," he said with an embarrassed grin. Clearing a space on the desk, he placed the ledger down and turned it round for Bone to read.

Bone opened the book and, flicking through to the most recent entries, he tracked them in reverse chronology. Halfway up the page, his finger stopped.

"Who's this?" Bone tapped an illegible scribble.

The clerk leaned over the desk and twisted his neck to try and see. Bone spun the book round impatiently.

"I'm not sure," the clerk said. "Monday twenty-seventh…" He pushed his glasses up the bridge of his nose. "I've only been on a couple of days. This is from last week." He scrutinised the scribble again. "I believe that says R. Gallacher? What a terrible signature."

Bone glanced down at the entry again. "What did he request?"

"I really don't know."

"For fuck's sake, I haven't got all day," Bone snapped. "I'm in the middle of a major criminal investigation."

"Let me write down the entry number and I'll check for you," the clerk said, and quickly copied down the six-digit number. "I need to use the computer, sir."

"So records are filed in a book by hand and recorded on the computer?"

"That's the system. I know it's pretty archaic. I think it's to do with a single point of failure or something like that."

"Just do it!" Bone demanded.

The clerk scurried off through a door at the back of the reception, and Bone continued to go through the ledger. A few minutes later the clerk returned, flushed and slightly out of breath.

"Okay, so sorry it took so long. I had to request a new password and—"

"What did Detective Superintendent Gallacher request?"

"Sorry. Yes, he signed out some personnel records."

"For whom?" Bone returned.

"I wrote down the name." The man held up the Post-it note and started to read. "The Personal Record File..." He paused and looked up. "Detective Chief Inspector Bone. You, sir."

"Me?"

"That's what's been recorded."

Bone stared at the clerk for a second and then turned to go. "Find the Meiklejohn files!" He stormed out of the office.

TWENTY

Bone pushed open Gallacher's door with such force it smashed against the adjacent wall. He was about to launch into an accusatory rage when he spotted a smart-suited woman sitting in a chair by the DSU's desk.

Gallacher sat back in surprise and cut Bone off before he could even start. "DCI Bone, this is Special Investigator Tennyson. She's from Edinburgh Central."

Bone glanced over at Tennyson, who stood and gave him a curt nod.

"Tennyson? Really?"

"I'm afraid so. Sarah Tennyson. My colleagues call me Saint Mirren," she replied without a hint of a smile.

Bone eyeballed the tall stranger with the styled crew cut who matched his gaze with equal ferocity. "To what do we owe the pleasure of a visit from Internal."

"Sit down, DCI Bone," Gallacher ordered.

Bone slowly lowered himself onto the chair opposite, his brain primed for wherever this was heading.

"As a special investigator for PIRC, I have been ordered by the procurator fiscal to investigate a complaint that has been made," Tennyson began.

Bone detected the purring twang of a Morningside accent. *Public School,* he thought. The upturned blouse collar peeking above her suit jacket was conclusive evidence of probable privilege, to him anyway.

"A complaint about what?" he snapped.

She reached into her bag and removed an envelope. "I have been ordered to serve you with a conduct notice," she said, her lip curling around the hint of a smile.

"What?" Bone raged. "What for?"

"As I said, a complaint has been made, and we are following standard procedure, DCI Bone," Tennyson continued.

"Let me guess who's complained?" Bone rolled his eyes.

"We are not at liberty to share that information."

"Well, it wouldn't take a police detective to work it out. I assume that's why you've been sniffing around in my personal records?" Bone shot his boss a withering look.

"We have concerns about your handling of the case, DCI Bone," Tennyson cut back in before Gallacher could reply.

"I thought we were talking about a specific complaint?" Bone replied, adding, "and I think you'll find that's 'sir', Special Investigator Tennyson."

"You have recently returned to work following a period of sick leave, is that correct?"

"So this is an interrogation now?" Bone fired back.

"DCI Bone. The SI is here to ensure that the current investigation proceeds quickly without any unnecessary change of leadership," Gallacher finally piped up.

His attempt at reassurance was lost on Bone. "The investigation is proceeding and will continue to proceed if you stop wasting my time here."

"I will need to interview you and your team, but I have no intention of obstructing the investigation," Tennyson said.

"*My* investigation, Ms Tennyson. We're all kind of busy trying to catch a cop killer, in case you hadn't noticed."

"I'm afraid you have no choice but to cooperate with me. When investigating a matter directed by the Crown and Procurator Fiscal Service, I have the power to interview, question, detain, arrest, and report for prosecution," Tennyson persisted. "And that's Special Investigator Tennyson, sir."

"Farce." Bone stood.

"Sit down, DCI Bone," Gallacher insisted. Then he turned to Tennyson. "Thank you, Special Investigator Tennyson. DCI Bone will instruct his team to cooperate fully with your enquiries."

Tennyson nodded and, picking up her briefcase, she left the room.

"What the fuck is going on, Duncan?" Gallacher said, launching his first verbal missile.

"I could ask you the same question," Bone snapped back.

"First you threaten Robert Meiklejohn's father, and then you accuse Chief Officer McLean — the victim's grieving bloody husband — of domestic abuse, and I'm not even going to mention the headline in the *Chronicle* this morning."

"So which one of these delightful pillars of our community has sent over Miss Jean fucking Brodie?" Bone couldn't help himself now.

"I warned you to keep the lid on this. I thought you were ready, but clearly this case is too much for you and a return to work was too soon."

"Meiklejohn and McLean are persons of interest. We are doing our job, clearly something you've forgotten how to do."

"Don't push it, Bone. You have no idea what pressure I'm under keeping you on this case. It's not just your neck, you know."

Bone sat back down. "Sir, I'm fearful that this copycat lunatic may strike again soon. We are pursuing this case as fast as we possibly can to try and stop the bastard. If you pull me now you'll upset the whole apple cart with the team, and the case could run off the rails."

"Forget the apple cart, Duncan. As far as I can see this is already a fucking train wreck." Gallacher slumped down at his desk. "You just need to calm down and lay off McLean. He is gunning for you. And I won't be able to stop him or any of his hired assassins."

"We have evidence of abuse."

"Where is this coming from?"

"PC Garvey's colleague, who happens to be one of her best friends."

"It's circumstantial. You know that, and McLean most certainly knows that, too. And if the press, who seem to know our every fart, get wind of your harassment of the victim's husband, they'll tear this unit apart."

"When I agreed to come back, you promised you would let us do our job in peace. Human shield, you said," Bone replied.

"This is fucking Hiroshima, Duncan. Just leave it be with the prosecutor, please."

Bone shook his head. "I'd better go and tell the team that Mary Poppins will be dropping in to waste the little time we already have."

"Just cool the bloody beans, okay?" Gallacher warned.

Bone slammed the door behind him.

When Bone broke the news to the team that Internal had landed, he was careful to emphasise that it was his nuts that were in the monkey wrench and no one else's, but his colleagues weren't having it. Mullens immediately declared nothing short of World War Three on Edinburgh Central, explaining in graphic and disturbingly gory detail what he would like to do to them all. Bone was grateful that they rallied round, but the pressure on the investigation was mounting, and they were rapidly running out of time. They needed a breakthrough, and soon, before the world came crashing down around them. Turning down the heat on Meiklejohn and McLean, as Gallacher had insisted, was therefore not an option.

He asked Baxter to check McLean's phone records on and around the night Garvey had disappeared and look for any recent dirt on Meiklejohn.

"But keep it low-key, okay? We don't want to ruffle any more feathers, not for now at least."

He approached the board and scanned the well-ordered spider's web of images, suspects, and clues again, hoping for a miracle. There was something he was missing that he couldn't quite grasp. He glanced up at the police mugshot of a youthful Meiklejohn, taken a few years before his pièce de résistance. He turned to Baxter.

"Check through Meiklejohn's prison records and get me the names of his cellmates and visitors."

"All of them?" Baxter's eyes widened in horror.

"A complete list," Bone replied. "This might go back farther than we think."

***

Within an hour of Bone's initial encounter, Tennyson had summoned him for interview. She was set up in one of the interview rooms, an attempt at

156

intimidation, Bone mused. When he entered, Tennyson was perched behind a desk, facing the door. She smiled curtly and invited him to sit opposite, in a chair she'd positioned just beyond the desk.

"I won't keep you longer than necessary, DCI Bone," Tennyson said, her hand poised over a tablet, the screen illuminating her face.

"Go on," Bone snapped back, taking his seat and pulling it in towards the desk to counter the intimidation.

"You were signed off sick last June, when you sustained a serious head injury following an explosion, is that correct?"

"You know that's correct," Bone said.

"And you led the team in the Robert Meiklejohn murder case?"

"Yes! Jesus."

"So when you received a parcel in the post containing a recording of the death of PC Garvey, it must have caused you some distress."

"Look, I haven't got time to play these games," Bone retorted.

"The police medical report states that you suffered from severe PTSD caused partly by the brain injury."

"Here we go." Bone sighed.

"How is your PTSD now?"

"Ask my counselling team."

"We have. I wanted to ask you."

"Off the scale right now. I don't know what I might do," Bone snarled.

"I'm just trying to establish your state of health, DCI Bone."

"Mental health."

"On Tuesday this week, you visited John Meiklejohn, is that correct?"

"He is a person of interest. My colleague and I went to his property, if you can call it that, as part of our ongoing enquiries."

"What happened there?"

"We asked him some questions. We left."

"And did you threaten or physically manhandle the suspect in any way?"

"An excellent suggestion, but no. We conducted our interview with the utmost professionalism, Special Investigator Tennyson."

"And then you interviewed Chief Officer McLean?"

"It wasn't an interview."

"An interrogation?"

"We had received information concerning his marriage and relationship with his wife. We needed to clear up a few things."

"With a grieving, distraught husband. Do you think that is professional?"

"It is what we are trained to do," Bone replied. "Investigate potential leads."

"And did you persist in your interrogation even though Mr McLean asked you to leave his property?"

"Don't call it that. It wasn't a fucking interrogation."

"Do you often lose your temper, DCI Bone? Is that one of the symptoms of PTSD?"

"Very good. Ten out of ten. You're wasted in Internal, you should come and join us in RCU. We'd be delighted to have you."

"Just one final question for now."

"For now? Is there going to be more of this shit?"

"I have explained my role to you, DCI Bone. When I am satisfied that I have sufficient detail, I'll be sure to let you know." A hint of a smile curled on her lips. "In your professional opinion, why do you think this so-called copycat killer has such detailed knowledge of the case, and why do think they sent the recording to you?"

"That's two questions, in my professional opinion."

"Doesn't it strike you as rather odd?"

Bone shook his head, and then the gears clicked into place. "Oh, I get it." He laughed loudly at the absurdity of the thought. "You think I'm connected to this in some way, is that it?"

Tennyson continued to type notes into her tablet.

"In my post-traumatic and highly aggressive state, in one of my fruit-loop moments, I decided to bury a colleague's wife alive." He stood. "And perhaps I was behind all the other murders and framed Meiklejohn, an innocent victim of my psychosis. And now I'm in need of another murder fix. Is that it?"

"That's all for now, DCI Bone. If I need to talk to you again, I'll let you know," Tennyson said, returning to her tablet.

"And I'm sure Advocate McLean would be more than happy to act as prosecuting counsel in my trial and finish what he's started here," Bone added.

Tennyson looked up and smiled again. "Thanks for your cooperation, DCI Bone."

TWENTY-ONE

Momentarily forgetting about the press camped outside the station, Bone exited the front entrance, and reporters lunged towards him like a screaming pack of ravenous hyenas, their cameras flashing and popping. He pushed his way through as the hysterical hacks jostled for position and fired questions in a simultaneous roar of white noise. Once again, McKinnon was right at the front.

"Are you losing control, DCI Bone?" he shouted through the cacophony. "Are you stable enough to lead the investigation?"

Bone grabbed the collar of McKinnon's grubby wax jacket and pushed him with full force back into the rabble. The man stumbled and fell sideways onto the path. Some of the journos turned and snapped him lying prostrate on the ground, flailing around and making the most of the drama. Someone pushed Bone from behind, and he surged forward through the press pack and quickly out the other side onto the road.

"This way," Walker said, now leading Bone.

They marched to a nearby car, with journalists on their tail, then jumped in. Walker locked the doors.

"See that? Central locking. It's a new thing that cars have these days," she said, starting up the pool car Audi. She pummelled it into first, leaving reporters stumbling after it in its wake.

"Thanks," Bone said.

"What were you thinking, pushing that reporter?" She slammed the car into third.

"Not just any reporter — it's that dung maggot, Colin McKinnon, from the *Chronicle*."

She drove on at speed across town and out towards Braebank Loch.

"Where are we going?" Bone asked.

"Coffee break," she replied.

When they reached the near side of the loch, she pulled into the car park. She climbed out, and he followed her down to the water's edge. The diminutive loch was completely still, the surface like a perfect pane of glass and framed by a line of gentle green hills, a far cry from the hullaballoo they'd both just escaped. Walker jumped down onto the tiny pebble beach and took in a long, deep breath. After a few more mouthfuls of cleansing oxygen, she turned to Bone.

"What's going on?" she asked, finally.

"I think that bastard, McLean, has called in his Gestapo."

"On you?"

"Yes!" Bone kicked a pebble across the beach.

"Can I be straight with you?" Walker continued.

162

"I wouldn't expect any less."

"I've known you a long time and I've never seen you behave so irrationally."

"It's been a tough few days."

"What did you expect? This was always going to be a nightmare, but dealing with nightmares is our job. That's what we're trained to do, day in, day out."

Bone knelt and picked up a flat stone. "Maybe Gallacher was right and I'm not ready." He skimmed the stone across the surface. The pebble bounced four or five times, creating multiple ripples across the loch, then sank beneath the surface.

"If you think that then you should walk away."

Bone looked up. Walker was still staring at him.

"I'm serious."

He watched the ripples melt back into the water. "I can't do that." He picked up a second stone.

"And why is that?"

"I need to end what never got ended."

"Exactly, and that's why you need to keep the heid." She tapped her forehead. "I can't believe I'm telling you to keep the heid. What is it you're always telling us?"

"Emotion is the enemy of the investigation," Bone replied.

"That's right, and you're behaving like an emotional dickhead." Then she added, "Sir," and smiled. She glanced towards a wooden hut at the far end of the car park.

"My shout," she said.

The tiny wooden café was deserted and decked out with half a dozen cheap plastic tables and chairs. They sat, and a young bearded man with long, unkempt hair emerged from the back of the hut, looking a little startled.

"Good morning, Fergus," Walker said as he approached their table, the pungent odour of herbal cigarettes wafting in behind him.

"Detectives," he said with mild horror. "What can I get you?"

"I'll have what you're smoking," said Bone.

"What's that?" Fergus replied with panic in his eyes.

Walker stepped in to save him. "Two coffees, both black, one with two sugars."

"Aye, no worries," Fergus said, and returned to grapple with the coffee machine.

Moments later he was back, and placed their drinks gently on the table. He lingered for a moment as though about to say something, then with a rub of his eyes, he retreated out the back.

"Drink it," Walker ordered.

Bone took a sip. "Thanks." He looked up. "God, that's good."

"The best wasted barista in town."

"No, I mean thanks for this."

"I'm only saying what you already know."

"Arshooz?"

"Number one." Walker smiled and took a drink. "Christ, you're right. I wonder what his cakes are like."

"Illegally good, probably."

"I've been thinking about our two suspects again, and to be honest, I'm unconvinced about either of them." Walker returned to the day job.

"Unconvinced?"

"About their guilt." She put the cup down. "Meiklejohn is just a sad and broken old alcoholic lunatic, and McLean — well, granted he is a nasty piece of work, and there's no doubt in my mind that he was abusive to his wife, but there's just nothing there that screams he killed her."

"What if he's trying to frame me?"

"What?"

"That's the reason, well, one of the reasons, I was so worked up. That investigator from Edinburgh practically accused me of setting the whole thing up."

"That's insane."

"Not if the prosecutor-in-chief is feeding them the line that I'm unhinged."

Walker stirred her coffee.

"And he might have somehow roped in Meiklejohn, using him in some way," Bone continued.

"Wow, that's quite a theory."

"Sometimes you have to push it out as far as it will go before you know how far you have left to bring it back in."

"Incredible."

"What?"

"The incomprehensible bollocks that comes out of your mouth sometimes, sir," she joked. "So what now?"

"We quietly keep digging into McLean's history."

"But if you think he's framing you, how are you going to stop it before he takes us all down?"

"The truth will out. It always does."

"I'm just not sure you're right about McLean's motives. I think his behaviour might be more about guilt and covering up for his misogyny. But like you say, worth digging around in that shite-on-a-stick's past. He needs stopping whatever way it goes."

They finished their coffees, and Fergus re-emerged from the back looking even more wasted.

"Cheers. Have a great day, officers," he said with a wide dreamy beam.

"And you," Walker replied.

She and Bone got up to leave.

"I'm pretty sure he's got an ultraviolet veg patch going on up there," Walker said, pointing at the loft hatch as they walked out.

"Well, I'm not going to be the man who stands between potentially five years and the best coffee in West Stirlingshire, are you?" Bone smiled.

"So the heid is back on?" Walker tapped her temple again.

"Momentary loss of signal. Hard-faced bastard cop is back."

"Okay, glad to hear it, sir. But more pasty-faced, if you want my honest opinion."

"We'd better get back to it before anyone else completely fucks up this case."

"It's a question of honour to see which one of us can do that first," Walker replied.

Back at the car, Bone's mobile rang. He listened for a moment then turned to Walker. "It's Baxter. She's got the name of a former inmate who shared a cell with Meiklejohn for nearly two years."

"Do we know where this person is now?"

"Guess?" Bone said.

Walker started the car.

TWENTY-TWO

In contrast to the 70s carbuncle of Kilwinnoch police station, Braefells High Security Prison at the arse end of Falkirk was the equivalent crumbling Victorian carbuncle, designed by Presbyterian psychopaths to exact the most physical of punishments the church could bestow on any living creature. In recent years, the Scottish Prison Service had attempted to modernise it to avoid a complete rebuild, but the result was not so much a polished turd but a skid mark of excrement, unfit for even the most inhuman of humans. Bone rang the security buzzer marked, 'Guests Only' next to a reinforced steel-panelled door.

"Okay?" Bone glanced over at Walker, who seemed a little apprehensive.

"I hate prisons," she said with a grimace.

"They aren't designed to be loved," Bone replied. "Especially this one."

The buzzer screamed and hissed, and a voice cackled through the tiny speaker.

"Sorry, I missed that," Bone said.

"You need to press the button when you speak, sir." Walker pointed at the panel.

Bone tried again.

"Name and prisoner you are visiting, please," the voice cut through the static.

"DCI Bone and DI Walker, here to see Derek Grechan."

The buzzer screamed again, then the door clunked, clicked, and swung slowly open. A burly prison guard in a Bri-Nylon white shirt appeared.

"ID, please," he said sternly.

Bone and Walker dutifully held up their lanyards. The guard scrutinised them for a moment, then ushered the pair in. They followed him along a narrow corridor completely encased in steel caging. Approaching airport-style security, Bone recognised one of the guards at the X-ray machine.

"Bob, how are you?" Bone asked and placing his rucksack in a tray and emptying his pockets.

"Ah, Inspector Bone. You're looking well, all things considered," the burly officer said, nodding at Bone's scar. "What brings you to the Hotel California?"

"We're to see Derek Grechan."

"Oh Jesus, that is one nasty wee bastard. Good luck with that." Bob the guard pulled a face.

"We need some information, and I'm hoping to oil the wheels," Bone glanced down at his bag.

The guard smiled, pushed the tray through the X-ray, and had a quick word with the other guard scrutinising the screen, before waving Bone through the scanner.

"All clear, Inspector," Burly Bob said, and handed him his bag. "Collect the rest on the way out."

"Cheers, Bob. I owe you."

Burly Bob sneered. "Enjoy! Can't say I envy you."

They followed the first guard farther into the bowels of the prison. When they reached a third door, he punched in a code, and they continued on. Another cage gate led them into an atrium with cells at various levels on either side and a mezzanine floor supported by exposed girders bolted on to the Victorian brickwork that teetered precariously above their heads. Strangely, there were no prisoners around.

"Where are the inmates?" Bone asked.

"Lunchtime in their cells," the guard replied.

They crossed the floor, through a fourth security gate and on into an austere, windowless visiting room with tables and chairs set out at regular spaces, and clear screens separating tables in two. Harsh strip lights ran the length of the room, filling the space with a brutal, yellow-white light, giving the visiting room the ambience of an abattoir.

"Take a seat, I'll bring Grechan down." The guard disappeared through the gate.

"Nice," Walker said, glancing around.

"I don't get the impression rehabilitation is high on anyone's agenda, do you?" Bone sat down at the nearest table. He removed his notebook from his backpack.

Walker joined him, and for a moment they sat in silence, taking in the ambience while they waited for Grechan to arrive. A couple of minutes later, the cage rattled, and an unkempt middle-aged man in a sweat top and sagging tracksuit bottoms stepped into the room, flanked by the prison officer and one of two more guards who had joined the party. They brought Grechan over.

"Sit down, please," Bone said without making eye contact with the inmate.

"Fuck sake, what happened to your scone?" Grechan nodded at Bone's injuries. "Are you gonnae turn into one of a they Terminator 2 blobby bastards in a minute?"

"Behave, Grechan," the guard interrupted.

"What's all this about? I didnae request any visitors," Grechan grumbled.

"This isn't a social call," Walker said. "We want to ask you a few questions."

"I'm done talkin' to you Percys. I'm no sure I can take the smell."

"Watch your mouth," the officer repeated and, leaning over, he prodded Grechan's shoulder.

"That's okay, Officer," Bone cut in, and gestured for the guard to back off. He reached into his bag again and produced a pack of cigarettes, then a second, and placed them on the table.

Grechan's eyes widened. "How did you...?" he asked but stopped when Bone placed a third pack on the desk and smiled. Grechan slowly slid into the seat opposite.

The guard positioned himself about six feet directly behind him, near enough to manhandle him if necessary.

"I'm DCI Bone, and this is DI Walker," Bone continued.

Grechan sneered at Walker. "I like the company you keep, Inspector."

Bone removed one of the packs of cigarettes and pushed it back into his rucksack. Grechan huffed and shook his head.

"You're in for murder and multiple counts of GBH, is that right?"

"Self-defence," Grechan retorted.

"You murdered three members of the same family on the same night," Bone added.

"It was a kill-or-be-killed situation."

"In two thousand and eight, you were convicted of assault and battery and served two years at Balmalloch prison."

"What? That was ages ago," Grechan replied. "Some bam chibbed me one in a pub."

"Don't tell me, self-defence?" Bone cut in.

Grechan shrugged.

"During your time at Balmalloch, you shared a cell with Robert Meiklejohn, is that correct?"

The colour instantly drained from Grechan's face. "What about him?"

"How did that go?"

"I don't like to talk about him."

"We understand he's not the nice guy you are."

"Don't compare me to him," Grechan rapped back. "I might have a bit of an anger problem, but he had a human being problem. The way he went on gave me the fuckin' wullies."

"Do you know if he had many visitors?" Walker asked wearily.

"His old man used to come to see him," Grechan said. "I remember him, cut from the same heidbanger genes."

"Nobody else?"

Grechan eyed up the cigarettes, and Bone returned the pack to the pile.

"He had a girlfriend, if you could call her that."

"Really?" Walker said.

"Aye. I know. Hard to believe. She'd visit him quite a lot. He called her something. What was it…" He stopped to think. "His vessel, that was it. Fuckin' weirdo. He used to talk about her to me. Say all kinds a nasty stuff. He said he was openin' her up like a can a sardines."

"He was going to kill her?" Walker interrupted.

"Naw, well, I dunno, maybe he did when he got out. No, he meant get into her heid, feed her his nonsense, you know? Like brainwash her."

"What did he tell her to do?" Bone pressed.

"No clue, probably pure skankin', whatever it was. He used to read out some of the letters she wrote to him. Jesus Christ. Said she'd fuck anyone or anything for him. He'd laugh his heid off. He was fuckin' her over good style."

"Can you remember her name?"

173

"He never said her name, just called her The Vessel."

"What did she look like?"

"Young lassie, way too young for him, and right bonny, but seemed a bit…"

"A bit what?"

"Like a left-footer."

"A Catholic?" Bone asked.

"Naw, a lezzer, ken?"

"A lesbian?" Walker clarified.

"Aye."

"And how exactly does a lesbian look?" Walker added.

"Och, ye know, just had that 'into women' kinda thing going on wae her."

"Excellent, thanks for clearing that up," Walker replied curtly.

"I always knew the heidbanger would murder somebody someday," Grechan continued.

"Takes one to know one, does it?" Walker snapped.

"So how long did this go on between them?" Bone cut in.

"Dunno, he was transferred after eight months."

"But at least eight months, then?"

"Oh aye, at least. Plenty a time to turn her into a total bunny boiler."

"And nobody else visited him?"

"Not that I know of. He wasn't exactly Mr Popular, ken?"

Bone stood. "That's all for now."

"Is that it?" Grechan replied. "So no pardon, then?"

The prison officer by the door approached.

"Well hello, darling, did you miss me?" Grechan taunted the officer, who ordered him to stand.

On his way round the desk, the inmate snatched up the packs of cigarettes and stuffed them into his tracksuit pockets. As he left, he let out a loud squeal like a pig caught in a meat grinder, then belly laughed and followed the guard back to his cell.

TWENTY-THREE

Back at the station, Harper called Bone over to his desk.

"A couple of days ago, I sent the records office a reminder email to fish out the Meiklejohn files, including the videos," Harper said. "Well, I just got a reply from Sam Tozier?"

"Aye, that's right. He's in charge down there, or at least he should be," Bone replied.

"There was no message, but he'd attached two files," Harper said. "A PDF, and this." He was about to click the file but stopped, his finger poised over the keys.

"Go on then," Bone urged.

Harper opened the file and hit the play button.

A video rolled on Harper's screen. The image seemed abstract at first, and Bone cocked his head to try to decipher what he was seeing on the screen. Then he realised. It was a close-up shot of a head wrapped entirely in black tape, with a horrifyingly familiar left eye exposed and blinking furiously. Within a few seconds smoke filled the screen, accompanied by the sound of muffled screaming. And then moments after that, tiny flickering flames appeared around the edges of the duct-taped head, the moans escalated, and the fire intensified until the head was completely alight, the surface of the tape peeling, and falling away to expose melting skin and bubbling flesh beneath; a gaping mouth, an exposed blackened cheekbone, and an eyeball sizzling and shrinking like a mushroom in a frying pan.

Bone reached over and stabbed at Harper's keyboard. "Stop it!" he cried.

Harper hit the button.

Harper looked up at Bone, who was holding his face in horror.

"Is this another?" Harper asked, shell-shocked.

"You said there was a PDF?" Bone said finally.

"Er—yes," Harper stuttered.

"Well, show me then."

Harper shook himself from his stupor.

Finding the file, he downloaded and opened it. It was a photocopied image of Sam Tozier's police ID, and underneath it were the words *Peek-a-boo, Yoo Hoo Two!*

"Vicious, evil bastard!" Bone hollered.

"What's up, sir?" Walker asked, approaching him.

"You'd better let Rhona see it," Bone said to Harper. "I need some air."

Up on the roof, Bone slammed the fire escape door. It bounced out of the lock and swung back open, so he slammed it again and again, then kicked it. He stormed over to the edge of the building and leaned out across the railing. After a few moments of raging at the sky, he turned back to the station. A figure lurked in the shadows by the air-conditioning unit. He approached, but the shadow seemed to retreat farther behind the metal casing.

"Who's there?" he called out.

"My old friend," the figure rasped.

Bone immediately recognised Meiklejohn's familiar, nasal-thin voice.

"I'm not your fucking friend!" Bone shouted at his hallucination.

The creature craned forward into the light, exposing its bomb-charred skull, partially concealed beneath a pit-black hood.

"You're in my head!" Bone shouted.

"Who are you talking to?" Walker's voice broke his unwelcome trance.

He spun round. She stood directly behind him, peering into the gloom beyond.

"Rhona. Jesus," Bone exclaimed.

"Who are you taking to?" Walker asked, peering into the dark.

Bone rubbed at his throbbing temple. "My conscience." He took a deep breath. "I take it you've watched it, then?"

"Horrific," Walker replied, taking a second squint towards the back wall. "Records confirmed Sam Tozier emailed in sick last Thursday, five days ago."

"What did he say was wrong with him?"

"Migraine. Of all things."

"Does he have a partner?"

"I've no idea but I'll find out."

"We'll also need to trace his movements on the days he was off." Bone slammed the fire exit door again. "Fuck! We need to stop this maniac. Right. Fucking. Now."

Bone stormed back into the station, and with one final glance across the rooftop, Walker followed him down.

Gallacher's reaction to the devastating news was strangely muted, and to Bone's relief, Tennyson was nowhere to be seen. But he assumed it was only a matter of time before the dogs would be called in. So for now, they ploughed on with the investigation, more determined than ever to nail the bastard and stop the killing.

In the hours that followed, Harper was tasked with going through Tozier's home laptop for clues to his movements before he'd disappeared. But his search uncovered some unsettling details about Tozier's private life. A search history revealed that Tozier was a frequent visitor to a site called *The Pet Shop*, which turned out to be an infamous dogging portal, where 'like-minded' romantics could share nocturnal extra-curricular pursuits.

When Bone and Walker had interviewed Tozier's distraught partner, she'd told them that Sam had gone fishing on the night he had disappeared, something she'd said he did once or twice a month, depending on the weather. But Bone suspected that his night-time fishing adventures were about something rather different than landing the big catch.

"Christ, his poor partner," Walker exclaimed when Harper filled them in.

"Aye," Bone said, turning to the incident board. "Not exactly a ringing endorsement for the male of the species, eh?"

"So could Tozier have stolen the Peek-a-boo files because he was being blackmailed?"

"Certainly a strong possibility," Bone agreed. "Tozier had a lot to lose." He turned to Harper. "You mentioned somewhere nearby where local doggers meet up — is that what they're called?"

"You're thinking of the LA dodgers," Mullens joked.

"The Foresthills car park, sir," Harper replied.

"That's very knowledgeable of you, Will." Mullens grinned.

"Locations are listed on Tozier's computer, and anyway, it's common knowledge, isn't it?"

Mullens rolled his eyes.

"The nature reserve?" Bone cut in. "It's beautiful up there. What kind of sick people would do that to such a special place?"

"Bloody dog owners," Mullens jumped back in.

The car park was quiet, with just two cars and a white van parked up facing a breath-taking view of the Campsie valley.

"Is it just me, or does this place feel a bit bleurgh?" Walker asked.

"Sadly, yes." Bone got out.

Walker followed. The white van started up and drove out of the car park.

"Something I said?" Walker joked.

They split up. Walker headed towards a parked Fiesta by the rear fence, and Bone made a beeline for the shelter. As Walker approached the vehicle, the front passenger window opened a crack, and a plume of thick smoke streamed out, followed by a pungent whiff of weed that smacked her in the face. She tapped the windscreen. Inside were two tracksuit-clad neds. Walker pushed her ID against the glass, and after a few seconds of panicked shuffling and shifting around, the window slowly unwound all the way down.

"Good afternoon, lads," Walker said. "What are you doing?"

"Er — whit?" one lad said, trying to get his lips to coordinate with his brain.

"What's going on?" Walker clarified.

"We're just enjoyin' the view," the lad continued.

The second lad coughed.

"I see. So you wouldn't be participating in a lewd act together, would you?"

"Whit?" the first lad replied in shock, while the second one's cough intensified.

"You do know this area is under police surveillance?" Walker lied.

"Right, er — naw, we didnae." The lad shook his head but now looked as though paranoia was getting the better of him. "We'll head, then."

181

"You do that, but before you go…" Walker interjected.

The lad stared straight at her, expecting the worst.

"You two weren't up here last Sunday night, were you?"

"In the night?" the lad asked.

"Around say, midnight?"

"Jesus, naw. I wouldnae come near here at night."

"So you're not into that sort of thing?"

"Whit do you mean? Christ, naw." The second lad laughed nervously. "That's pure rank."

"But, that camera up there—" Walker pointed vaguely towards the trees "—might think you *are* into that sort of thing. So if I were you, I'd bugger off now before I have you done for possession, okay? And tell your dopehead mates to stay clear as well."

"Shite," the first lad said. Winding up the window, he started the engine, spun the car round, and screeched out of the car park as fast as his clapped-out banger would go.

Walker continued to the farthest corner, then while turning back to find Bone, something crunched under her feet. It was a tiny bottle — an injection vial.

"Junkies," she mumbled. She peered closer to read the information stuck to the side. *Shit.* She whistled for Bone, who emerged from the shelter and marched over. "Propofol." She pointed at the vial.

"Sicko sex game?" Bone said.

"Or forced sedation?"

"I'll call in the site team. I think we might have found Tozier's favourite fishing spot."

TWENTY-FOUR

Approaching the incident room, Bone spotted Baxter coughing in the corridor on her way back from her twice-hourly pilgrimage to the Temple of Golden Virginia. When she saw him, she waved.

"Sir," she choked.

"Have you got that list of Meiklejohn's visitors yet?" Bone cut in.

"Yes, and it took me bloody ages. Scottish prison service is about as efficient as a Scotrail trolley service. I've found something else of interest, too." She nodded enthusiastically. "McLean's phone records have thrown up something interesting." Her voice cackled down the corridor.

"Shh. Jesus." Bone pointed to Gallacher's office.

"Sorry, sir."

Together, they went back to the incident room.

At Baxter's desk, she opened the spreadsheet.

"So, first of all, I checked the visitor records between the dates Meiklejohn served his time at the jail, and for a seven-month period he received frequent visits from a woman called Jennifer Bailey."

"How frequent?" Bone asked.

"Weekly, sometimes twice weekly."

"So do we have anything on her?"

"Not a thing yet, which is very odd. I literally can't find a trace of her existence other than her name on the records."

"Keep looking."

"Of course." She smiled. "Now McLean." She switched screens and opened another file. "I checked his calls around the Tuesday night, and he made three to the same number, at six thirty-seven, eight-twelve, and then again at eight thirty-three. That last one was over an hour long." She scrolled up. "Then when I went farther back, that number kept popping up."

"Is it a work number?"

"No, it's a mobile, registered to an address in Bearsden."

"And a name?"

"Yup," Baxter said triumphantly. "A Ms Claire Shaw."

"Does she work in his firm?"

"No, I checked that, too. She used to work for a small marketing firm but left four years ago."

"Okay, I think we need to find out who this Ms Shaw is."

"Will, job for you," Bone called over.

Harper, who had his head buried halfway into his keyboard, almost jumped out of his seat with surprise.

"I need you to drive over to McLean's house and keep an eye on his movements. Use your own car."

"Me, sir?"

184

"Yes, you."

"Watch his house, in my car?"

"Bloody hell, Will. It's called policing. I'll fill you in sometime when we're less busy."

"Like a stakeout?"

"If you say so. Just park up at a discreet distance and write down when he arrives, and then if he leaves, follow him."

"Yes, sir," Harper said, trying to contain his excitement.

"He doesn't know you, and you don't exactly look like a cop, especially in that defibrillator you call a car."

"You can talk," Mullens interrupted.

"I'm on it, sir." Harper beamed.

"And ring me if he's on the move, okay?"

"Sir." He hurried back to his desk, grabbed his jacket, and dashed out.

"Mark?" Bone continued.

"Aye?"

"You do the same for Meiklejohn, but make sure you aren't spotted — which I know is an impossible request. A blind man in a blizzard would see you coming."

McLean's mystery caller's semi was located in a leafy avenue on the outskirts of Bearsden, one of Glasgow's more salubrious suburbs. Walker parked up the nondescript station pool car three or four doors away, and Bone clocked the property.

"Let's sit tight for a bit and wait for signs of life," he said. After twenty minutes or so, he blew out his cheeks and opened the door. "You stay here and keep an eye on the street."

He approached the house slowly. The blinds on the ground floor were drawn, but there was a full bottle of milk on the front doorstep. He sidled up the path and squinted round the side of the house where a Nissan Micra was parked up in a covered car port. He rapped the door and stood back. No response. He was about to rap again when his phone rang.

"Bugger," he muttered. Fumbling in his coat, he quickly answered.

"McLean's coming," Walker warned.

"Buggerations." He dived into the car port and ducked behind a bin, just as a champagne-white Mercedes pulled up.

McLean emerged clutching a garage-purchased bunch of flowers. He flattened his errant locks with his palm and marched up the path to the house. Bone ducked lower. The door opened before he reached it, and a woman appeared with an infant dangling from her arms. McLean extended the flowers, but she attempted to shut the door, so the advocate stuck out his foot, forced it open, and disappeared inside.

Bone crept out from behind the bin and, edging round to the front widow, leaned in to listen. For a moment all was silent, but then came voices — a woman shouting, followed by McLean's bellowing baritone. Bone couldn't make out what they were saying, so he moved closer to the door and pressed his

186

ear to the surface. But with a loud click, it swung open. He jumped back. The door slammed shut with force. Quickly, he retreated behind the bin.

The door thumped and rattled on its hinges as though someone was either trying to open it or keep it shut. He was about to return and knock, fearing McLean was having a go at the woman, but it flew open again, and McLean stormed out followed by his bunch of flowers, which hit him square on the back of the head. Ignoring the impact, he retreated to his car, with a single rose still clinging upside down to his hair. The woman slammed the door, and with a screech of tyres, McLean drove off at speed up the street. When the coast was clear, Bone emerged from behind the bin and returned to Walker, who was anxiously waiting in the car.

"Looks like our honorary gentleman has a mistress who doesn't seem that enamoured with him."

"The slimy shit," Walker said.

"And there's a kid, too." Bone rolled his eyes.

"His?"

"That's for us to find out. Come on." Bone climbed back out of the car.

"We're going to see her?" Walker said in surprise.

"Of course."

"But shouldn't we keep a low profile in case McLean gets wind?"

"I'm not particularly in the mood for backing off from that repugnant human being, are you?"

Walker smiled and followed him out.

After a couple of knocks, the door flew open.

"I told you to stay away!" the woman hollered, but when she saw the startled detectives, her face fell. "Oh, sorry," she flustered.

"Good afternoon. I'm DCI Bone, and this is DI Walker. Is it possible to have a word?" Bone held up his ID.

"Sorry, who?" the woman said, her face smeared with mascara. She was significantly younger than McLean, possibly in her late twenties.

"We're from Kilwinnoch station," Bone added.

"What's this about? I've got my son. I need to…"

"It won't take long. We'd just like to ask you a couple of questions."

"Why — I mean, have I forgotten to pay for petrol at the garage again or something?"

"No, nothing like that. It's just part of an ongoing investigation. We just need to clear up a couple of things. Can we come in?"

"Er…" She looked at them both suspiciously.

Walker gave her a reassuring smile, and she ushered them in.

"Sorry to disturb you," Bone said as they negotiated the hall strewn with a multitude of toys. "Could you confirm your name for us?"

"I'm Claire Shaw."

"Thanks."

She took them into the living room, which was in the same devastated state. The boy was over by the TV, drawing on the wall with a giant, blood-red crayon.

"David, no!" Claire shouted. Dashing over, she snatched the crayon out of the boy's hand.

He started crying.

"Sorry," she said.

She disappeared for a moment, leaving Bone and Walker with the screaming boy.

"Is that a house you've drawn there?" Bone pointed at the mess on the wall.

The boy stopped crying for a second and eyeballed Bone, then he resumed his ear-shattering wail.

"That went well," Walker whispered.

Claire returned with a KitKat and, breaking off a finger, handed it to the boy, who instantly stopped screeching, stuck the stick in his mouth, and slurped loudly on the end.

"Please sit down," the young mum said.

Bone glanced round, but all the seats were overflowing with toys and toddler-related debris.

"Oh jeez," the woman said, grabbing toys, teddies, and handfuls of Lego bricks, and dropping them on the floor.

Bone and Walker sat, but Walker jumped back up when something squealed under her. She reached down and plucked a toy clown out of the armchair, then placed it down on the carpet.

"So, as we said, we are conducting enquiries as part of our investigation," Bone continued.

"How can I help?"

"Do you know a man called Ross McLean?"

The woman's expression seemed unsure of which emotion to express.

"No, I don't think..." she began, her voice quivering. "I don't know him, no," she said unconvincingly.

"Ms Shaw, we saw Mr McLean leave your property ten minutes ago," Bone pressed.

"Oh, Mr McLean?" the woman said with mock surprise. "He just called in as he's helping me with...the possible purchase of a property."

"Mr McLean is not that kind of lawyer."

"He's a friend of the family."

"Does your lawyer often bring you flowers?" Walker asked.

The increasingly distraught mum looked at Bone then Walker, then back at Bone, and tears welled.

"It's okay, Claire. You can talk in confidence," Walker said.

Unable to contain her emotions, the woman sobbed, and her head fell into her hands. Bone glanced over at Walker, gave her a discreet nod, and got up.

"Sorry, Ms Shaw, I have to take this call," he said, finding an excuse to let Walker press her gently. He weaved around the mess and went out into the front garden.

"I just don't want to do the wrong thing," Claire mumbled through floods of tears.

"That's okay, take your time." Walker smiled.

"I'm so tired of it," Claire continued.

Walker fished a clean handkerchief out of her pocket and handed it to her. "So how do you know Mr McLean?"

The woman wiped her nose. "It was never meant to be like this, my mess of a life."

Walker sat quietly and let the woman offload.

"I was doing fine. A great job, friends…and then *him*." She spat out the word.

"What happened?"

"This happened." She glanced over at her boy, whose face was now almost entirely covered in melted chocolate.

"We met at a conference four years ago. I wasn't even at the same one. I was at my company's annual do."

"What do you do, Claire?"

"I used to work for a small marketing firm. I loved it." She bit down on her lip.

"So this was a hotel?"

"Yes. His do was a much more extravagant affair. Free bar, fine dining, band, disco. Me and my colleague crashed it." She blew her nose. "You know what these things are like? Too much booze and everyone out of their comfort zones. The next thing you know, I'm chatting to Advocate McLean, chief prosecutor for the whole of Scotland." She winced when she said his name. "Or rather, he was talking at me, and I fell hook, line, and sinker for his bullshit." She stopped, sighed, and continued. "So then one thing led to another, and my life changed forever."

"Is the boy his son?"

She looked up. "What has he done?"

"We're just trying to establish the kind of man Mr McLean is."

"Oh, I can tell you that." Claire scowled. "He's a first-prize prick. Yes, that's his son. He denied it at first, even made me take a DNA test."

"You might want to…" Walker said nodding to the boy who was now smearing chocolate on the TV screen.

"David!" the mum exclaimed again, but he continued to ignore her. She shook her head. "You see? I didn't know he was married, I really didn't."

"I know, it's okay," Walker replied.

"And he bloody lied about it for months. I was so stupid. His wife is listed on bloody Wikipedia, for God's sake."

"So did he give you a hard time, then?" Walker guided her gently around another emotional precipice.

"At first he thought he could just shut me up. His dirty little bit on the side," Claire raged. "But I know my rights, and Chief Officer Ross McLean is pretty familiar with them, too. To be honest, I didn't want his scummy money, but I'd lost my job and I was on the brink of losing this house, so I agreed to monthly payments."

"And did he stick to those?"

"Oh, at first, yes." Claire stopped again.

"It's okay, you don't have to say."

"No, I want to," Claire said. "But then he started to impose certain conditions, and if I complained, the payments stopped."

"What sort of conditions?" Walker asked, though she suspected she already knew what was coming.

192

"Oh, you know, I had to be nice to him." She grimaced. "Usually around a time when his wife was out for an evening."

"Awful." Walker shook her head.

"And when I refused he would get aggressive and threaten to cut the money or worse. He literally had me over a barrel."

"Does he hit you?"

"No, but he's come very close. And when I told him I didn't want his money anymore, I thought he was going to kill me or David. He scares me. He's a nasty piece of work."

"We'll stop this, I promise." Walker took the mother's shaking hand. "I can put you in touch with an organisation that will help and support you."

Claire whimpered again.

"Would you like me to do that?"

"I just want to be free of him."

"You will be," Walker said and gently squeezed her hand. "Would you like me to ask a liaison officer to pop round?"

"I'll be okay. He won't be back today."

Walker stood. "Okay, I'll be in touch with the next steps."

The mum joined her, the load on her shoulders now appearing a little lighter.

"If he comes back later today or any time, ring me right away." Walker handed Clare her card. "You're not alone anymore. We've got your back."

"Thank you." Claire gave Walker a tight hug.

"I'll see myself out," Walker said.

The young mum returned to her son who was re-enacting Bobby Sands' dirty protest on the curtains.

Outside, Walker inhaled deeply and blew out a long puff of anger.

"Well?" Bone asked.

"I'll fill you in back at the car." She sighed again. "I need a minute to calm down."

TWENTY-FIVE

Reaching over to the back seat, Mullens grabbed his coat and rummaged in his pockets, desperately seeking something to eat. Nada. *Shite.* He searched the inside pockets. Still nothing. *Bloody starving.* He checked the glove compartment in front and then the side pockets of the car door.

"Bingo!" He pulled out a half-eaten packet of Rolos. "Thank you, God," he said, and rammed two in his mouth at the same time. "And thank you, whoever had the car out last." A long string of caramel-coloured saliva dribbled onto his suit.

"Foacks ske," he mumbled, and then squeezed another two in, his cheeks now bloated like a hamster.

There was one left. *Would you love someone enough?* he thought. *Bloody right I do.* He pushed the last one into a tiny space remaining in his left cheek. Munching and slurping, he checked Meiklejohn's ramshackle excuse for a house at the top of the lane, but there was no sign of him, or anyone else for that matter.

Swallowing a sweet shop of liquidised sugar, he climbed out of the car and headed up the lane. When he got to the gate, he hunkered down behind a crumbling dry-stone wall and clocked the house again. Picking a lump of toffee from one of his gold-crowned molars, Mullens looked up on hearing a noise. Someone was moving around behind the house. Moments later, a plume of smoke appeared above the rooftop, and the crack and spark of a fire was obvious.

Keeping low, he ventured farther in. When he reached the side of the house, he quickly cut across the yard and dived behind a rusty trailer with one of its wheels missing. Edging forward, he caught a glimpse of Meiklejohn dumping objects onto a bonfire. Meiklejohn disappeared, and then moments later he was back with more junk that he tossed into the flames. Mullens moved closer to try and see what Meiklejohn was burning, but his phone rang.

"Shite!" he mumbled and, fumbling in his suit pocket, he snatched his phone out. It was his dad again. *No!* He accidentally answered instead of cancelling the call. Meiklejohn spun round from his burning pyre.

"Who's there?" he shouted, on the verge of venturing to look. But then he shrugged and continued emptying the contents of drawers on to the pyre, followed by the drawer itself.

"I'm on a job, Da," Mullens whispered down the handset.

"I'm stuck in the loo, son."

"Not now, Da."

"I'm desperate," his distraught father moaned.

Mullens glanced over at Meiklejohn, who was now leaning on a cane, staring at the roaring pyre he had created.

"You're stuck in the loo now?" Mullens asked, annoyed with himself for getting drawn in.

"Not in, on."

"Oh, Jesus Christ," Mullens moaned. "Can you no ring Bill to come round and help you?"

"Who?"

"I give up." He retreated round the side and back down to the car. "Hold on. I'll be there in a few minutes."

"Hurry, son, I cannae feel ma legs."

Mullens hung up, started up the car and backed down the lane.

When he got to his father's house, the door was unlocked, and he let himself in.

"Da?" he called out.

"In here," his dad cried from upstairs.

"Aye, I know where your bloody loo is," Mullens called back, and bounded up the stairs two at a time. He tried the door, but it was locked. "Da, can you let me in?"

"I'm stuck on the loo, how the fuck can I let you in?"

"Awright, awright," Mullens replied. "I'm going to have to jemmy the lock."

"Well, don't bloody break it," his dad warned.

"Okay then, I'll just limbo myself under the crack, shall I?"

"There's no need for that," his dad huffed.

"Right, keep back."

"Are you havin' a laugh?" his dad cried out.

Mullens gave the door a hard nudge with his snow plough shoulder, and the door flew open, the lock and shards of doorframe flying in and scattering on the floor at his dad's bloated bare feet.

"I told you no to break it."

"So I'll just leave you in here then for the sewer rats to climb out the pan and chew at your gonads."

Mullens surveyed his dad's predicament. His father's massive arse cheeks were bulging over either side of the loo seat, his legs turning a deeper shade of purple before Mullens' eyes.

"Jesus, Da, just stand up and pull your trousers up."

"I cannae, son. I'm stuck solid. When a flushed the loo, I think I must have created some kinda vacuum, and my arse has been sucked in." His dad looked up at him like a lost wee boy, his face flushed from trying to escape from the loo's angry jaws.

"How long have you been here?"

"About an hour. I thought if I left it a wee while, that might break the seal."

"You're unbelievable," Mullens despaired. "C'mon, let's get you up."

He put his arms around his dad and heaved. Nothing budged. If anything, the suction intensified.

He tried again. Both of them huffing and puffing for a few jerks and pulls, but still no result.

"Wait," Mullens said. He searched the bath for his dad's back brush.

"A bit of leverage," he said, ramming the end of the brush between his dad's legs.

"Hoy, sir, watch the crown jewels."

Mullens twisted and turned and jack-handled the brush back and forth, and with a hiss and a fart, he managed to squeeze some air between his dad's butt and the toilet seat.

"Right, let's try again," Mullens said and, dropping the brush, he wrapped his arms around his dad's shoulders and heaved him with full force off the seat.

With a loud pop, they both flew backwards and down with an almighty thump onto the bathroom floor. Mullens' dad landed like Giant Haystacks on top of the flushed Mullens, their straining faces pressed together. For a second or two, they lay there panting with relief that the nightmare was over. But then slowly they disentangled like a couple of stranded giant turtles waiting for the tide to return. Mullens' dad rolled over and toppled onto his back, his nakedness now fully exposed to all low-flying planes. Mullens sat up and, grabbing a towel, threw it over his dad's modesty.

"Ma legs are still kaput," Da said.

"My patience is bloody kaput," Mullens cut back. "You need help, Da, I mean professional help."

"I'm no getting no bloody nurse or care worker in. They'll clean me out."

"That's their job."

"Naw, I mean they'll rob me."

"You've nothin' to rob."

"I just don't trust them."

"But I can't keep comin' round at all hours. I'm a busy detective, you know? We're in the middle of a case."

"I'll no bother you again. I'll soon be out of all this anyway."

"Oh, for God's sake, Da. Come on," Mullens said and, taking most of the weight, he helped his dad up. "Hold on to the rail and wipe your arse."

"I can do it myself."

"I've already seen it all, pal, and trust me, Brad Pitt will be sleepin' easy tonight."

His dad cleaned himself up, and Mullens helped him pull up his pyjama bottoms.

"Right. Wash your hands, and I'll make you a cup a tea."

"I'm okay now. You go back to your car chase or whatever it was you were doin'."

"Tea first, c'mon."

Together, father and son shuffled through to the living room. Mullens lowered his dad on his support chair and turned on the TV. By the time he got back with the tea, his dad was fast asleep, snoring like a blocked drain.

TWENTY-SIX

"Hey, Columbo?" Bone said, prodding Harper in the back.

Harper unglued his face from his computer screen and spun round.

"Thanks for warning us McLean was on his way."

"What?" Harper replied.

"Never mind."

"I did follow him, though. He left at ten forty-three, and I tailed him to the High Court—"

"Tailed?" interrupted Bone. "The lad's out for ten minutes and he's dirty bloody Harry."

"He went in, and I was there about an hour, but then I left. I just assumed he was there for the day."

"Or not." Bone shook his head.

"While I was out on the road," Harper continued. "It was a bit odd, but I'm pretty sure a car followed me there and then all the way back to the station."

"And *Miami Vice* is back in the room," Bone joked.

"I'm serious, it was a white vehicle — you know, the French bubbly one?"

"The French bubbly one?" Bone replied sarcastically. "Have you thought about another career path?"

He turned to Walker and pulled a face. "White Citroen — the bubbly one?"

"C3?" Walker added.

"Thank you, Detective Inspector Walker. Good job." Bone smiled. "Are you absolutely sure about this, Harper?"

"Definitely. I noticed it a few minutes after I set off after McLean, and it was right behind me the whole time."

"Sir?" Baxter interjected from her position by the window.

Bone and Harper went to join her.

"Like that one there?" She pointed down into the rear car park.

A white Citroen was parked up near the entrance.

"Exactly like that!" Harper replied with surprise.

"So who's the owner?" Bone asked.

"That's the investigator's car," Baxter confirmed. "I've seen her arriving and leaving in it, you know, when I'm out for a..." She grabbed her smokes. "Excuse me a minute," she said, sucking in her cheeks as though searching air particles for residual nicotine.

"Is it now?" Bone fumed. "SI Tennyson is seriously starting to break my bloody balls."

"Sir," Harper cut in.

"What?" Bone snapped back.

"I've been putting together a montage of PC Garvey's movements that night using the CCTV footage from shops on the high street. I'm nearly done, but Scotsave gave me these." He held up a VHS tape.

"Good God," Bone exclaimed. "I thought I was the only one in the town with a penchant for retro. You probably don't even know what that is."

"I do, because my mum's old VCR is still at the house. I've got some equipment to transfer the tape to a USB. Is it okay if I head home and do that now?"

"Sure. Go." Bone gestured.

Harper grabbed his things and left, and Bone marched out behind him.

For the second time in a week, Bone pushed Gallacher's door open with such force it almost fell off its hinges.

"Where's nippy sweetie on steroids?" Bone growled.

"Who?" Gallacher stepped back from a filing cabinet, still clutching a file with papers precariously peeking out of the sides.

"Special Investigator Tennyson."

"We set her up in one of the empty offices on level two. What's happened now?"

Bone stormed out, and the papers from Gallacher's file gave up the fight and scattered to the floor.

Tennyson was sitting at a desk pushed against the rear wall of a near-empty office. Her laptop was open, and her mobile rested by its side. When Bone entered, she glanced up calmly as though she was expecting him.

"What are you doing following my detective?"

"I beg your pardon?" Tennyson said politely.

Bone wasn't fooled. "This morning, you followed DC Harper."

"I'm conducting an investigation into serious allegations against you and the RCU. I am doing my job, DCI Bone."

"And then there's the CCTV footage that you tried to get your hands on. Is it part of your remit to undermine my investigation?" Bone growled.

"I will do whatever is necessary to ensure an accurate and faithful report is presented to the procurator fiscal, DCI Bone."

"You've travelled so far beyond the line you're in cloud cuckoo land. What is your game?"

"I don't play games," Tennyson snapped back. "Why was your detective following Chief Officer McLean?"

"That's a police matter, and discussing the case could put lives at risk. You'll need to take that up with my chief," Bone replied, attempting to stonewall her.

"I'll find out one way or another. I have access to everything from here." She pointed at her laptop.

"You do that. Knock yourself out. But if you stick your beak in one more time, I'll be on to the chief constable faster than you can say prime fucking suspect."

Shortly after Bone's tête-à-tête with the investigator, a familiar face appeared at the incident room door.

"Is DCI Bone here?"

Mullens disengaged momentarily from his tussle with a crisp packet. "Dr Widowmaker!" he exclaimed.

"Widdowson," the station's criminal psychologist clarified.

"Things must be bad if you've turned up." Mullens' packet of crisps exploded all over the floor. "Sir, our resident shrink is here." Kneeling, he scooped up handfuls of Salt & Shake and returned them to the bag. "They'll no need much shakin' now," he joked.

Dr Widdowson winced.

"I know I'm probably the last person you want to see," Dr Widdowson said before Bone could speak, "but your chief asked me to have a look over the case, and seeing as I was involved with the Meiklejohn investigation, I thought I should have a word."

"Gallacher called you in?"

"He did, yes."

Bone shook his head. "I don't know what part of 'I'm in charge of this investigation' people aren't getting."

"Sorry, I've clearly stepped into something." Dr Widdowson raised his hands.

"No, I'm sorry. It's been a trying day."

Bone ushered him into his office, a room he rarely used. "Excuse the mess." He pushed a pile of boxes away from the doorway and cleared a chair of debris so that Widdowson could sit down.

"When I heard you were back, I was very pleased," Widdowson said.

"How so?"

"Denial or exclusion from a chosen life path is fraught with problems. Short-term, you did exactly the right thing, but longer term, it was important for you to reconnect with the life choices that make you happy and satisfied."

Bone nodded.

"And how are you coping?"

"Are you here to talk about the case or my case? Has Gallacher sent you here so you can report back on my state of mind?"

"Of course not. I'm asking as a concerned colleague, not as a shrink."

Bone squinted at him suspiciously. "I'm fine, thanks for asking," he said briskly. "So, you've read through the case file?"

"Yes, it would appear we have a killer at large who is attempting to replicate in some way the Meiklejohn murders, is that correct?"

"A copycat."

"I've always found the term copycat a rather odd way to describe imitative behaviour. I own three cats, and aside from genetic replicative patterns, they rarely actually copy each other. They present dominant behaviour traits that are unique to them, as we would expect in all sentient beings."

"Your point is?" Bone said, already a little frustrated with Widdowson's verbosity.

"They say imitation is the sincerest form of flattery, but my point is that attempting to mimic or replicate behaviour patterns in order to flatter your hero or heroine is extremely dangerous. It often leads to failure, frustration, disappointment, and ultimately, resentment."

"And mass murder?" Bone interrupted. "The two cases have significant differences."

"Yes, and considering all the evidence so far, in my view, you are dealing with a deeply disturbed narcissist — a fantasist who is projecting their own sense of worthlessness into hero worship behaviour."

"It's a dangerous game putting people on pedestals."

"Hero worship syndrome is a mental illness, and this individual is mentally disturbed. That's why I needed to speak to you so urgently, Duncan. I believe this individual will kill or attempt to kill again. Their desire to emulate and 'worship' is compulsive, but is inevitably self-defeating. The kill will never satisfy because the imitation will always be flawed, and so the cycle continues."

"That's what keeps me awake at night." Bone sighed.

"The question is — why is this killer hero-worshipping Meiklejohn? What has triggered their obsession?"

"Revenge?"

"Hero worship syndrome is akin to delusional obsession, where the worshipper believes that they are an indispensable figure in the life of the worshipped, and their love or fanaticism gives them some kind of biological and spiritual bond above all others."

"Like a stalker."

"Correct, and if this individual believes that his or her hero was killed unlawfully or unfairly, and taken from them, then vengeance can often become a prime motivator."

"Could this be a setup? I mean, could someone be faking this obsession to hide a different kind of revenge?"

"It is possible, and I could be wrong, but in my view, this is textbook hero worship syndrome. It is too extreme to be some kind of facsimile. The falsehood would quickly crumble under that kind of sustained pressure."

"Thanks, Graham, that is very helpful."

"A word of caution, though, Duncan."

"Another one?" Bone smiled.

"The longer this individual exists inside the fantasy bubble they have created for themselves, the more deranged, damaged, and desperate their behaviour will become." Dr Widdowson stood. "They need to be stopped, and sooner rather than later." He gave Bone a friendly nod. "I'll see myself out. It's good to have you back, and if you need my help again, you know where I am."

Bone returned to the incident room, with Widdowson's warning still ringing in his ears. While his love of psychologists had taken a serious hammering over the last year, he knew in his gut that Widdowson was right. The most important piece of this grotesque jigsaw puzzle was still missing, and if they didn't find it soon, another officer would most certainly die.

TWENTY-SEVEN

On his way back to Corstorphine, Harper checked his wing mirror every few seconds, but there was no sign of Tennyson's Citroen. Pulling into the narrow gravel driveway of his hobbit-like sixties bungalow, he glanced up at his inheritance and sighed. When his mother had passed away, his first thoughts had been to sell up and move nearer to Kilwinnoch and his work. A posh retirement bungalow on the outskirts of Edinburgh wasn't exactly the girlfriend magnet he was hoping for. But after a couple of months of living there on his own, without his mother continuously nagging him, he got used it and secretly began to like it, though he'd never admit that to anyone, especially his work colleagues. So now, eighteen months on from his mother's death, he was still there, still surrounded by her belongings, still driving her old Honda Jazz — or as Mullens called it, the Zimmer frame on wheels — and still without a girlfriend.

Inside, Harper fished out his mum's old VCR from the bottom of her wardrobe, still rammed full of her clothes and vast collection of shoes. Carrying the old machine through to the living room, he set up the equipment, plugging in cables and connecting his laptop to the twentieth-century device. When he was finished, he paused and made himself a coffee, using the percolator his mum had brought back from her holiday in Tuscany just before she'd died.

Back at the VCR, he turned everything on. The VCR whirred and clicked, and his laptop sprang to life. Fishing two tapes out of his briefcase, he pushed the first into the slot and pressed play. The machine juddered, and then finally a scratchy black-and-white image appeared on the screen. He turned the screen for a better look. It was an aerial view of the side road, adjacent to the Scotsave car park, taken presumably from the roof of the supermarket. The counter in the bottom corner read 10:23 p.m., Tuesday 28th September. The image appeared to be static.

Harper skipped forward to 11:35 p.m. and continued to play. Same scene, no movement. But then, in a quick flash, a car sped past. Harper rewound and played it again, but the glimpse was too fleeting for the ancient technology to capture, and the paused image deteriorated into static fuzz. He ejected the tape and inserted the second. This time, the video was taken from the opposite side of the car park, by the entrance, with a clear view of the entire front of the car park. The quality of the recording was a little clearer, too.

Harper skipped ahead to the critical time. PC Garvey stumbled into shot and staggered across the car park. A car appeared in the entrance, approached, circled her, and stopped by her side. Harper leaned in closer to try to identify the make and model.

"Shit," he gasped, recognising the distinctive bulbous shape of Bone's Saab immediately.

He continued to watch, his mouth open. The car crept after Garvey. She stopped and turned. The passenger door swung open. Garvey stepped back, tripped, and fell sideways. The driver's door opened, and a figure jumped out, ran around the car, and knelt by her side, and then after a moment, helped Garvey back to her feet and into the passenger seat. The car set off towards the entrance gate. It stopped, and the driver glanced up towards the camera. Harvey rewound and replayed, and repeated again, pausing on the critical moment. The tape flickered, but this time the primitive technology delivered, and the driver's features were clearly visible.

"Oh shhhhit!" Harper stammered.

He turned at a sudden thump somewhere behind him. He jumped up and scanned the room. A second thump, came from the back of the house. Pressing the eject button on the VCR, he grabbed the tape, dashed into the hall, and squeezed the tape behind the boiler in the airing cupboard. Then, creeping into the kitchen, he picked out the biggest kitchen knife he could find from the cutlery drawer and slipped back down the hall, through to the rear of the house.

With the blade primed, he tapped open the spare room door, but it was empty. He checked his mother's bedroom. Nothing. At the end of the hall, he pulled the back door, and to his surprise, it opened. His security routine every morning and evening was obsessive, so leaving the door unlocked when he was at work was not in his DNA. He leaned in and scrutinised the lock. The doorframe was split around the socket, with clear signs of forced entry.

He stepped out into the back garden and scanned the boundary fence. All was quiet. Stepping back in, he shut and double bolted the door and returned to the living room. He glanced down at the VCR. The second tape was gone.

"Phone!" his mind screamed, but before he could turn, he was grabbed violently from behind.

He raised the blade instinctively, but a gloved hand twisted his wrist until the bone cracked and the knife dropped to the floor. Another hand, round his throat, tightened until he could no longer breathe. He kicked out, his foot connecting with a side table, sending his mother's precious ornaments flying. The assailant was now dragging him backwards towards the kitchen. At the door, he snatched at the frame, but then a chemical-soaked cloth was pushed into his face, smothering his airways in choking, odorous fumes.

Chloroform he deduced, but after a brief, futile struggle, he was unconscious.

TWENTY-EIGHT

At the bottom of the close, one of Bone's neighbour's kids was out playing on the stairs. He'd covered almost the entire landing in Lego bricks to form a toddler work of art fit for the Tate Modern.

"All right, wee man?" Bone said as he attempted to pick his way across the ocean of coloured plastic.

"This is my city," the wee lad said, placing another brick directly in front of Bone's left foot.

The boy's flustered teenage mother appeared at her door.

"Oh, dear God!" she exclaimed. "I'm so sorry, Duncan."

"No bother, Fiona," Bone said reassuringly, while still balancing precariously on one leg. "That's some town. I'd love to live there, Gregor."

But the boy was too engrossed in his town planning to respond.

"Gregor, let Mr Bone through." She dashed over and plucked the boy up from his multi-coloured metropolis so that Bone could pass.

The boy struggled and cried.

"God's sake, you've already wrecked the house with your mess and now you're out here," she complained. She pushed the bricks with the side of her foot and cleared a pathway for Bone to proceed.

"He's enjoying himself, and if he's out of your hair, then result." Bone laughed and negotiated his way up to the first landing.

"Aye, you might be right," she replied with a weary smile.

She put the boy back down, and he immediately started to repair the earthquake damage. Shaking her head, she returned to her flat.

"Your town needs an airport," Bone said to the boy, who stopped what he was doing, looked up, and smiled, then manically cleared a space.

When he reached his landing, Bone spotted a brightly coloured jack-in-the-box sitting on his doormat. *Sweet kid*, he thought, but as he knelt to pick it up, he spotted what appeared to be a tangle of wires wrapped round the outside, disappearing through a couple of drill holes on the front.

Fuck! Booby trap!

But he was too late. The lid sprang open, and with an ear-piercing scream, a cloud of ash exploded out of the top, like a mini volcanic eruption, showering him in a thick layer of grey dust. Coughing and spluttering, he put the jack-in-the-box down and frantically wiped at his eyes and mouth. Through the dust cloud, he squinted back down at the box. A toy clown dangled from a cloth-covered spring, with a strip of paper attached to the top of the clown's multicoloured bonnet. Bone knelt again and, rubbing at his stinging eyes, he read a small inscription written along the width of the paper.

Ashes to Ashes.

Farewell Sam

"Oh, dear God, no!" Bone said, shaking what he suspected to be Sam Tozier's cremated remains from his clothes and hair.

TWENTY-NINE

It was a typically dreich day for PC Garvey's funeral. As Bone parked up the Saab, the tragic irony of burying Garvey for a second time hit him for six, and he took a moment or two to recover his composure. He climbed out and approached the funeral party huddled around a canopy of black umbrellas. The minister, the Rev. Angus Macintyre — a familiar face from the many burials Bone had attended as part of his job, and a name to haunt the very soul of anyone thinking of not dying — was already in full-blown sermon mode, his ponderous prayer bouncing off the high walls of Kilwinnoch Parish Church.

Bone stood back discreetly and scanned the sodden sea of forlorn faces. McLean was next to the minister, juggling a prayer booklet with his umbrella, and next to him were some of Garvey's colleagues, faces Bone recognised from his interviews, including Sanjit Mohan, who nodded when he saw Bone arrive. Gallacher was there, too, in full formal uniform, but no one else from high command. And then at the end of the grave stood an umbrella-less and soaked to the skin Tennyson, who seemed to be ignoring the downpour entirely.

Bone moved a little closer. The minister completed his prayers, and McLean reached down, picked up a handful of clay, and threw it into the grave. Stepping back, he glanced up and spotted Bone hovering in the background. Garvey's colleagues then followed McLean's lead and tossed more fistfuls of soil into the grave. The minister stepped around the covered mound of excavated earth and retreated to the relative shelter of the side of the church wall. McLean followed him, and they spoke together for a minute or so, and then he broke away and approached Bone.

"I don't want you here," McLean said quietly, attempting to control his anger.

"I've come to pay my respects to PC Garvey," Bone replied.

"If you had any respect you'd stay away. Please leave," McLean said. He marched back.

Bone watched him for a moment as he resumed his conversation with the minister. They were joined by Gallacher. They spoke for a moment, McLean frowned at Bone and pointed, and it was Gallacher's turn to approach.

"Duncan, the Chief Officer has asked you to leave. I advise you to respect his wishes."

"I'm not here for him, but don't worry, I'm going."

"Such a sad day," Gallacher said before he returned to the graveside to talk with Garvey's colleagues.

On his way out, Bone cut across the cemetery, and on the far side by the open fields, he searched the rows of tombstones until he found the grave of PC Katie Edwards, Peek-a-boo's first victim. A freshly picked posy of flowers rested by her headstone, and it appeared as though someone had recently cleared leaves and weeds around it. He knelt to read the inscription.

Always in our hearts
Our beloved Katie
1991-2018

He turned at the crunch of shoes on gravel. It was DS Mohan.

"Sorry, sir, I didn't mean to disturb you," Mohan said.

"This is PC Edwards, she was Peek-a-boo's first victim. Two years ago this week."

Mohan studied the gravestone. "She was only twenty-seven?"

Bone nodded. "She had two kids. Her partner was destroyed by it. It was as though every bone in his body had been smashed to pieces. I hope they are all okay. I should check up on them."

"You did your very best, sir."

"Sometimes best doesn't cut it." Bone stood.

"Hazel said to me once," Mohan continued, "the most we can hope for is happiness."

"Why did she say that?"

"Oh, something daft had happened in the station, and she was being sarcastic probably, but I remember thinking at the time that she really meant it, and that was the way she was at work, always on the side of happy, for herself and for her colleagues. She was a good person, and that's what really counts."

"What I can't understand is why she would marry a prick like McLean." Bone shrugged.

"Insecurity, maybe. Who knows? She was way too good for him, that's for sure."

"Thanks," Bone said.

"What for?"

Bone smiled, and with a nod, Mohan went back to rejoin his colleagues.

THIRTY

Bone returned to his flat to rummage around in his homework files for Widdowson's original psychological profile reports. When he arrived, he checked his answer machine — four messages. He clicked through, and the first three were from Gallacher, with ever-increasing hysteria about his DCI's behaviour, but the fourth message was from Alice. He sat on the edge of the bed to listen. Her voice was calm and reassuring, as always. She said she'd been thinking about what he'd said and asked if he'd like to babysit on Friday night. When the message ended, he played it again. This was the crack of light he had been hoping for. Searching for his mobile, he rang her back, but there was no reply. He garbled out a grateful message but then deleted it and tried again, this time a little more measured, accepting her offer. When he hung up, a text pinged on his phone. It was from a private number. He opened the message.

Peek-a-boo!

His letterbox rattled, and he dashed to the hall. A white A4 envelope lay on the mat. He threw open the door, but the close was empty. He dived downstairs, taking two or three steps at a time, almost tripping and falling before he hit the ground floor and sprinted out into the street. Up ahead, he spotted a hooded figure in an all-black tracksuit running away from the tenement. He gave chase. The runner hooked down a side street, and Bone lost him for a second but then spotted him again, leaping over a garden wall.

Bone followed, though scaling it a little slower than his target. The drop on the other side was high, but after a split-second hesitation, Bone jumped down. The runner was now careering across a front garden and back onto the main road, heading down the hill towards the high street and shops. Bone pushed harder, and the gap was narrowing. At the top of the town, the runner weaved through shoppers, almost knocking a pensioner over, her bag of vegetables spewing out onto the road. Bone leapt over the bag onto the road and straight for the figure. He was within a few feet now. The runner took a sharp left and dived down a narrow cut-through leading to the library car park. Bone continued to pursue, but as he crossed the car park, a white van appeared from nowhere and tore straight at him.

Bone swerved to avoid impact; the driver slammed on the brakes and sounded his horn. Bone carried on, but he'd lost his mark. *Shite*. When he reached the other side of the car park, he scanned left and right, but still no sign. He stopped and gulped in lungfuls of air, his chest on fire. He looked back at the library entrance. Maybe the runner was hiding in there? He was about to check but then the van driver roared past, sounding his horn again and firing a slurry of swearing at him. Bone turned and spotted the figure again, this time in the distance, sprinting across the primary school playing field. Bone resumed the chase. When he reached the primary school perimeter fence, the runner leaned on one of the goalposts at the far side of the asphalt football pitch.

Bone ran to the school gate and attempted to climb it, but he couldn't get a foothold. He dashed back along the fence towards the runner, who was bent double, breathing almost as hard as Bone.

"Stop!" Bone hollered, his arms flailing, but knew fine well it was a pathetic order.

The figure straightened up, gave Bone the Vs, and with a hop, skip, and jump, he scaled the back fence and was gone.

"Fuck!" Bone panted, and then he coughed up a lung.

He fumbled for his phone, but he'd left it on the bedside cabinet.

Fuck! He coughed again.

When he got back to the flat, soaked in sweat and his whole body screaming in agony, he knelt to examine the envelope, a bestial groan pouring out of him as he moved. The typed address was identical to the killer's previous gift. He found his phone, called the station, and went to run a hot bath.

THIRTY-ONE

Once the SOC team had completely smothered Bone's flat in fingerprint dust, alongside Sam Tozier's dusty remains, the envelope was removed and taken back to the station. Bone and Walker went down to the lab to talk to the forensics officer who was tasked with examining the contents. The woman — stern-faced with fifties-style glasses — met the detectives in the small reception area.

"What have you found?" Bone asked.

"One set of prints on the exterior of the envelope," the officer said, and removing a set of surgical gloves. "But no match, unfortunately, though the size indicates that they belong to either someone with small hands or an adolescent."

"That would explain the Spider-Man impression," Bone said. "Just some wee lackey doing a delivery for a tenner, no doubt."

"What about the seal — any DNA?" Walker asked.

"Self-sealing, sadly."

"And inside?" Bone asked, bracing himself for what was to come.

"Have a look," the officer said, and she gestured for them to follow her into the examination room.

The envelope and contents were laid out like a body under another set of eye-straining LED lights that forensics seemed to corner the market in.

"So, inside we found another greetings card," the officer said.

Across the front the card read:

Sorry you're having to leave because your boss is an absolute basket case.

And beneath that was an image of a ghoulish creature emerging from a wicker picnic basket.

Bone glanced up at Walker.

The officer unfolded the card with a pair of tweezers. "We also found an unbranded USB that matches the spec of the one we examined last week. We have removed and examined the exterior shell, but again we have nothing," she added with a frown.

"Have you checked the contents of the stick?" Walker asked.

"That's not in our remit," she said.

"So where is it?" Bone asked, his impatience growing by the second.

"One moment please." The officer disappeared and returned a few minutes later with the tiny USB resting in her palm. "I left it under the scanner." She smiled.

"Is it okay to touch it now?" Bone asked.

"Of course, unless you are the sender and you're trying to cover your tracks," the officer joked, but it landed like a lead-filled souffle.

Bone picked it up and turned it over. "Can we take it, and the card?"

"Sure, we're all done here. But you'll need to sign them off."

She about-turned again.

"God's sake," Bone huffed.

"Sorry sir," she said, dashing back clutching an iPad.

"Damn thing." She flicked the on button back and forth but the pad refused to start. "Bloody cutbacks." She thumped the side impatiently. "Oh, just take them for now, I'll ask someone to sort this out."

Walker scooped up the envelope and card, and she and Bone left the room, the officer still grappling with her gadget.

Bone shut his office door, and the team gathered round the computer.

"I'm so sick of these horror shows," Mullens groaned.

Bone inserted the stick in the slot, opened the solitary, unnamed folder, and clicked the video icon.

"Here we go," he said, and leaned back.

The screen went black, and the upload wheel appeared and chased its little blue tail round and round for what seemed like a lifetime.

"Come on," Bone said impatiently.

Mullens tutted. "How old is your computer? I mean, look at it?" he said, the nerves getting to him.

"Quiet," Bone replied.

As the screen flickered, the speaker hissed, and an image appeared, but it was extremely dark, and the sheen from Bone's office window was making it worse. Baxter ran over and pulled the blind. On screen, in the middle of a gloomy room, a figure slumped in a hard-backed chair. The image flickered again, and the camera zoomed in closer. It was a man stripped to the waist, his wrists and ankles bound to the chair and his head covered by a hessian hood. A rough-edged circle was hacked out of the fabric, exposing the man's left eye, the lid opening and closing slowly. A tube, attached to the man's left arm, extended down to a glass container on the floor, the end pushed through the top, with liquid dripping slowly and collecting in a thick mass of crimson at the bottom.

"Oh my God," Mullens said. "Not another one."

"The shoes," Walker said.

The man was wearing a pair of trainers, the embarrassingly uncool and dirt-cheap kind an overbearing mother would buy a sheltered son.

"It's Will," Walker said.

Bone turned, scanning the distraught faces behind him, hoping to see Harper's flushed baby face.

"He's not here," Mullens said.

Bone's head dropped into his hands. The video hissed, and a distorted voice whispered, "Peek-a-boo". The hiss turned to an electrostatic scream, the screen returned to black, and the video ended.

For a couple of seconds, Bone and the team stared at the black mirror in shocked silence.

"Fucking evil bastard!" Mullens roared.

Bone jumped up. "Has he been in today?"

"No," Baxter said. "I thought it was a bit strange as you could normally time the migration of Canada geese to his daily routine. I just assumed he was still working on that footage at home."

Bone rushed out of his office and over to Harper's desk, with his colleagues in pursuit. "Where was he collecting this stuff? On his computer or a memory stick?"

"I really don't know," Baxter said, her face white and drawn with anxiety.

"Does anyone know his password?" Bone scanned his team's shell-shocked faces.

"IT will be able to unlock it," Mullens said, finally.

"Right, get on to them now. Harper is alive in the video, and we have to believe he's still alive, so we all need to focus. Sheila, can you get uniforms over to his house? Where does he live?"

"Edinburgh. It's his mum's old place," Baxter replied.

"Where's she?"

"Dead."

"Okay, get a trace on his phone and..." Bone paused. "Let Gallacher know. Mullens, can you go through the video again?"

"Aw, sir," Mullens moaned.

"Go through it again and look for anything that can help us save our colleague's life."

"Sir." Mullens returned to Bone's office.

"Rhona, we'll go to Edinburgh. Pool car, you drive."

THIRTY-TWO

Walker had picked a high-performance car with a siren, so their journey to Edinburgh would have given an EasyJet flight a run for its money. Bone had called admin for the address, and they arrived at the house just as three uniforms were climbing out of squad cars. One approached their car.

"We've just arrived, sir. Would you like us to seal the area?"

"Yes, front and back," Bone replied.

The detectives marched up the driveway.

"Car's missing," Walker said. There were two deep tyre marks in the gravel. "And someone's left in a hurry."

Bone stepped towards the door and was about to try the handle when he stopped. "Gloves?"

Walker reached into her coat and produced her own set. "Let me," she said. Slipping her hands in, she tried the door, but it was locked. She shifted round the side of the bungalow and pulled at one of the sash windows, but it was locked tight.

Bone peered inside. All was still. Walker tried a second window, but it, too, was tight as a drum. Leaning in, she hammered the underside of the frame with the balls of her hands, and after a couple of precise blows, the window slid open. Bone glanced over.

"Venture Scouts," she said.

Bone started to climb in.

Walker grabbed his arm. "Wait. What about contamination, our shoes?"

"No time." Bone continued on in.

Walker followed behind.

The kitchen was sparse but immaculately tidy.

"He's a very organised person," Walker said.

"It might just save him," Bone replied.

They scanned the room and moved into the living room.

"Look." Walker pointed at the upturned side table with smashed ornaments scattered around it.

Moving farther in, Bone spotted the VCR on the floor and a tangle of cables sticking out the back.

"That's where he was working on the Scotsave footage," Bone said. "He had a VHS tape." Kneeling, he examined the front of the machine. "Rhona…" He gestured for Walker to come over. "Is there a tape in there?"

Walker poked her gloved finger in the slot. "Empty."

They searched the room, but there was no sign of the tape.

"And no laptop?" she added.

"And no laptop either," Bone added. "Somebody clearly wanted to get their hands on that footage."

Walker pointed, "Bedrooms?"

But before they moved, there was a commotion at the front door. The locks clicked, clacked, and clicked again, and a police officer appeared in the doorway.

"Inspector?" the PC said, peering into the living room. "The neighbour has been round with a set of keys." He stopped. "Wait, how did you get in?"

"The back door was open," Walker cut in.

"Is the neighbour still there?" Bone asked.

"Aye. And she's a wee bit agitated, to put it mildly."

Bone turned to Walker. "Okay, check the bedrooms and bathroom. I'll go and speak to the neighbour."

Walker nodded and carried on down the hall.

Outside, an elderly woman, bedecked in a Harris tweed trouser suit not entirely dissimilar to DS Baxter's choice of fashionwear, paced up and down by the front gate.

"DCI Bone, ma'am. I'm a colleague of your neighbour."

"What's happened to Will?"

"Nothing to worry about. What's your name again?" Bone asked.

"I'm Mrs McGinnis, Mrs Jean McGinnis, twenty-four Meadowpark…"

"Oh aye, hello, Jean. Will speaks very fondly of you," Bone lied, hoping to help the pensioner calm down. "So you live next door, is that correct?"

"Right there, number twenty-four. I've lived here for sixty-four years. I knew Will when he was a wee laddie, and I used to sew the hems of his trousers. He had very short legs for his age."

"He still does." Bone smiled, reassuringly.

"I was a seamstress."

"A dying art," Bone said. "So when did you last see Will?"

"He's not been hurt or anything?" Her panic returned.

"Oh no. This is all just part of a separate investigation that Will's helping us with. So did you see him last night when he got home?"

She looked over at the house and back at Bone. "I saw the lights come on. He's fitted one of those home security things that goes off when someone moves about on the property, or…"

"And what time was that?" Bone continued.

"Oh, he's usually home at seven o'clock, regular as clockwork, but last night he was a bit later, maybe quarter past eight. I was putting my milk bottles out and I saw the car pull in."

"And this morning, did you see him leave for work?"

"Well, that's the funny thing. As I said, he's normally regular as clockwork. He's right fussy like that. But last night I was up as usual with my reflux. I get it something chronic, and it seems to be getting worse. I mean, I've done what the doctor tells me and—"

"So did you see him leave then?" Bone interrupted.

"Aye, well, I was in the kitchen getting ma antacid and I heard his car engine roaring like one of those noisy night flights coming in to Edinburgh airport. A right commotion, so it was."

"When was this?"

"Ach, I'd say just before midnight because I checked the clock on the cooker to make sure it was three hours since ma last antacid."

"And did you see him leave?"

"Ach, no. By the time I got to the window to see what was going on, his car was halfway down the road."

"Was he on his own?" Bone pressed.

"I didn't have my glasses on, but I think he was. He's not been having an illicit affair, has he?"

"No," Bone shook his head. "Was there anything else you noticed?"

"I did."

"What was that?"

"See that set of lights at the end there?" She pointed to the junction onto the main road. "He went right through them on red. Just not like him at all."

"Thank you, Mrs McGinnis. You've been extremely helpful. This lovely PC will see you back to your house now."

"I'm not an invalid," she huffed and, pushing past the PC at the gate, she disappeared into her house.

"Sir?" Walker called from inside.

Bone returned to the house.

She was upstairs in one of the bedrooms hovering over a side table.

Resting on top was a sheaf of notepaper with a column of names scribbled in pencil down the side, some with ticks alongside. Bone leaned over to look. It was a list of the shops on the high street.

"I asked him to go round the shops and check the CCTV for any footage of PC Garvey that night. That's what he was working on," Bone said.

"So these are the ones he's checked or still to check?" Walker asked. "But what's he done with all the footage?"

"Hopefully we'll find it on his work computer."

THIRTY-THREE

"Sir." Baxter marched over to Bone as he walked into the incident room. "Gallacher has been in three times looking for you."

"Bugger."

"You go, I'll carry on here," Walker said.

"Has digital forensics managed to get into Harper's computer?" Bone asked.

"Yes. I'm on it now, sir. We've found the CCTV footage he was collecting of PC Garvey's movements when she left the pub," Baxter replied.

"Can I have a look?"

"What about Gallacher?" Baxter asked.

"Gallacher hasn't been bloody kidnapped."

At Harper's desk, Baxter sat and logged in to the desktop. "His password is Obi Wanker Nobby." Baxter rolled her eyes. She searched the folders and retrieved the mp4 file marked 'Garvey'.

"I've had a quick run through, and Will has edited the footage to show Garvey's movements from the pub." She pressed play, and the video started up. "So this is from the roof of the Fells," she said.

The grainy black-and-white image showed a deserted street. Seconds passed, then Garvey appeared, wearing her duffle coat. She glanced back, took a left, then apparently changed her mind and walked back the other way. She disappeared out of shot, but then the scene clicked and changed to farther down the high street.

"And this, I think, is the shoe shop's security camera," Walker said.

Garvey staggered on, almost falling off the pavement.

"Shit, she was really hammered," Walker said, shocked.

The next camera picked up Garvey's trail at Dawson's Café, fumbling in her handbag. The footage switched again. The ironmonger's CCTV caught her shuffling past, then the traffic light camera captured her as she crossed the junction at the bottom of the town. She careered across the road, luckily deserted, and stumbled into the Scotsave car park. The video stopped.

"Is that it?" Bone asked.

"I think so. I can't find any more." Baxter flicked through the list of folders. "That's the part he was working on."

Bone scanned the incident room. "Where's Mark?"

"No idea," Walker said.

"For God's sake. We're under siege here, and he goes walkies."

Just then, Mullens walked in clutching an armful of calories. They all turned and stared at him.

"What?" he mumbled, his jaws chewing on something sticking out of his mouth. "I get hungry when I'm stressed."

"Mark, I need you to get down to Scotsave and find out if they have copies or backup or any kind of master file of the CCTV footage for last Tuesday."

"With their level of tech? I seriously doubt it," he said, dropping his skip load of saturated fats on his desk. "I mean, unless you're after recordings of Scotland's match with Holland in the nineteen seventy-eight World Cup. I'm sure they'll still have that battering about."

"Just go," Bone shouted. "Every second we waste here pissing in the wind, we risk losing Harper."

Mullens snatched up a family bag of chocolate eclairs, about-turned, and bolted out of the incident room.

Bone turned back to Baxter. "Keep searching Will's computer for anything else that will help us find him."

"Will do."

"I'll check on the progress at Will's house and see if his car's been found yet," Walker said.

"Okay, right, I'll go and try and keep Gallacher in his box," Bone said.

Gallacher was at his desk, but when Bone entered, he stood.

"What the fuck is going on?" he bellowed.

"DC Harper has been abducted, sir."

"Yes, I know, but seeing as you didn't bother to tell me, I had to find out from SI Tennyson."

"What the fuck is she sticking her oar in for?" Bone snapped. "I received another video through the door. We believe he's still alive, being held somewhere. It's another copycat. The bastard is slowly bleeding him, like PC Tyrrell."

"A second officer, and one of our own this time." Gallacher stared at Bone with fury in his eyes. "And now this on my doormat this morning." He tossed a newspaper across the desk.

Bone picked it up. A colour photo strip was spread across the front page showing Bone pushing over McKinnon outside the station, with the heading above in bold red letters

Crazed Cop Lashes Out

"It was a dive the Italian league would be proud of, sir. I didn't go near the weasel."

"I don't give a rat's arse for him either, but the public believe what they see, a cop losing control, and they would be right."

"Sir."

"You thump a pensioner. You accuse Scotland's top lawyer of wife battering, abduction, and murder. Our chief records officer is toast, and now you allow one of your team to be kidnapped. I would say that headline is pretty accurate."

"With all due respect, sir—"

"Respect?" Gallacher interrupted. "I don't see much respect for anything here — your job, your rank, the law, my trust in you. Where is it, Bone?"

"I told you we would do this my way, and you agreed."

"I didn't agree to intimidating powerful public figures or all the rest of this incompetent, and quite frankly, dangerous mess you are responsible for."

"Sir. We are on this."

"You said that before, and look where we are now, up to our gullets in shit river without a life raft, never mind a fucking paddle." Gallacher marched round his desk. "Have you any idea how difficult it was to get the DCC to agree to allowing you back?" He leaned in to within spitting distance of Bone's face. "My head was already in the guillotine, but now it's bouncing down a very steep slope into disciplinary and forced retirement on minimum pension."

"Our team will find DC Harper and catch this creature."

"Every time you say that things just get worse, Bone, so just shut it for once."

"Okay, what do you want?" Bone grumbled.

Gallacher returned to his desk and slumped down. "Two days, that's all I can give you. After that, you're off the case, and I'll recommend that you are unfit for active duty."

"Why don't you just sign me off now?"

"Don't fucking tempt me," Gallacher growled back. "I'm doing this because I owe you one last chance, as a friend. But after that, you are on your own, and I won't be there to stop them tearing you a new arsehole."

Bone was about to respond but could see Gallacher was beyond moving.

"And I'm sick of saying this, but back the fuck off McLean. He is *not* involved."

"Yes sir," Bone said, hoping Gallacher wouldn't spot the lie in his eyes.

He returned to the incident room with the desk sergeant following in behind him.

"Sir, sorry to interrupt," he said. "Paul Quinn is in interview room three."

"Who?" Bone asked.

"The groundworks labourer. Remember you asked us to bring him in for questioning?" Baxter called over from her desk.

"Oh bugger, yes, of course. Bone rubbed at his scar and tried to clear his head of Gallacher's raging rant. "Where's Rhona?"

"Gone back to Edinburgh. We might have a lead on Harper's car," Baxter added.

"Come on then," Bone said.

"What, me?" Baxter replied. "Really?"

"Yes, DS Baxter. Move it, before I change my mind."

She grabbed her bag and followed Bone out.

THIRTY-FOUR

Paul Quinn sat hunched over in his chair like a man awaiting lethal injection. Bone and Baxter sat opposite and stared at him in silence for a few moments to turn up the pressure.

"I dunno why I'm here. I've told you I didnae do anythin'," he said, squirming in his own stew.

"Looks like a guilty man to me, wouldn't you say, Detective Baxter?"

"Most definitely." Baxter nodded enthusiastically. She was revelling in the moment, free at last of her desk.

"Am I under arrest?"

"Oh, even more guilt. What would we arrest you for, Paul?"

"Well, if you're no goin' to arrest me, I might leave, then." He leaned back with a sudden surge of cockiness.

"Stay where you are," Bone ordered. "We'd like to ask you a few more questions, if that's okay with you?"

"I should have representation."

"Oh my, that's a big word," Bone replied. "How does the law stand on that, DS Baxter?"

He eyeballed Quinn again. "My colleague here is an expert in criminal law, you know, that thing you brush up against now and again?"

"That was years ago, I'm a changed man."

"You don't seem that different from where we're sitting."

"Mr Quinn came voluntarily to the station, so he can come and go as he pleases," Baxter said.

"Unless we arrest him?"

"Well, yes." Baxter nodded.

"Arrest me? Jesus Christ. I didnae kill that polis woman."

"And a man who leaves prematurely usually has something very serious to hide, wouldn't you say, Detective?"

"That is often the case, yes," Baxter affirmed.

Quinn's squirming intensified.

"So, Mr Quinn," Bone continued. "If you'd like us to continue to believe you are whiter than white, then I suggest you hang around a wee bit longer."

Quinn sighed and cowered back down behind the desk.

"So, when we met you on the seventh of October, you told us that the gate was already open when you arrived for work on Wednesday the twenty-ninth of September."

"Aye, that's right."

"Why didn't you say anything to the foreman? Didn't you think that was a bit odd?"

"No, like a told you. I just thought the council had forgotten to lock up."

"And then the day before, you were last to leave, is that correct?"

"Eh..." Quinn scratched his head. "I don't think so."

"Did you have your coat with you?"

"Oh aye, that's right, aye. I wasn't last out but I had to go back for ma coat. My smokes were in it."

"So the foreman gave you the key?"

"It was only a minute. I just dived in, grabbed my jacket, and was out again in two shakes."

"And you locked the gate again?"

"I did, and I gave the key back to Davie."

"Why didn't you mention this on the day we talked?"

"I forgot."

"But you now remember about your cigarettes?" Bone leaned forward. "That's quite a detail, considering how forgetful you are."

"I went back, got my coat, locked up, and gave back the keys, end of," Quinn replied and folded his arms.

Bone opened a file in front of him, containing a printout of Quinn's DSS record of employment.

"I see here, in your interesting and varied employment record, that in the summer of twenty thirteen, you were employed by Baird Construction as a labourer on a landscape job in Gatehouse of Fleet. Is that correct?"

"God's sake. I can't remember that. I've done a thousand jobs. I just take whatever I can get."

"Let me prick your memory," Bone said sarcastically. "You lived and worked on site between June and September, on the new bypass."

"Wait, aye, that's ringin' bells," Quinn said. "I didn't nick anything if that's what this is about."

"As if I would even suggest such a thing," Bone replied. "Can you recall who you worked with on that particular job?"

"No clue," Quinn said.

"So you all stayed together in a single static caravan for over six weeks and you have no recollection of any of your work colleagues?"

"Like I say, I just go where the work is."

"What about Robert Meiklejohn?"

"Who?"

"Come on, everybody knows Peek-a-boo."

"Aw, him?" Quinn's eyes widened. "Hold on a minute. I've got nothin' to do with him."

"That's not what your records say."

"He was a total weirdo. Everybody hated him. I was only nineteen, and he scared the shit out a me."

"You were acquainted then?"

"Listen, if you think *I* killed this polis woman 'cos he was my mate or something, that's just bollocks, total bollocks. I kept well out of his way."

"So going back to the day our local PC was brutally murdered." Bone kept up the pressure. "You left the gate open for when you returned later with the policewoman, who you'd drugged."

"No!" Quinn cried.

"You then started up the Bob Cat, dug a deep trench, threw her in, and buried her alive," Bone persisted, trying to push Quinn to spill the actual truth he was clearly hiding.

"Jesus, no!"

Bone turned to Baxter. "Detective, how many years can Mr Quinn expect for the brutal slaying of a well-loved local bobby and pillar of our community?"

"I would say, in my professional judgement, double life sentence."

"So Mr Quinn is likely to remain in custody until his death?"

"Correct," Baxter confirmed.

"Okay, okay," Quinn threw up his arms in defeat.

"I only thought they wanted to rob the supplies and maybe some of the ironwork."

"Who are *they*?" Bone pushed.

Quinn shifted uncomfortably from one side of his chair to the other.

"Who are *they*, Mr Quinn?" Bone repeated.

"I got this letter in the post with a hundred quid in it. It said leave the gate open and you'll get another ton."

"Who sent the letter?"

"I dunno."

"Come on, you expect us to believe that?"

"I'm tellin' you. A got a note and the cash. I just thought it was some gang, a local firm, you ken? The kinda folk you wouldn't ask who they were."

"And where is this note?"

"I burnt it."

"So you got a note from a total stranger with a hundred quid in it and you did exactly what this complete stranger said?"

"Two hundred notes, you know? It might not be a lot of money to you, but it's enough to keep me in my house another couple a months."

"And did you receive the next instalment?"

"Did I fuck." He looked up. "Anyways, dirty money. I wouldn't want it now anyway with that polis women lyin' in there." He put his head in his hands. "I didnae kill her, I just took the money for the gate. I would never have done it if I'd known."

Bone sat back. "My colleague and I will be checking your story in more detail. We will be in touch again in due course. You can be sure of that, Mr Quinn."

"Can I go?"

"For now, yes. But this is very serious, Mr Quinn, and you may be facing charges and a potential custodial sentence."

"So you don't think I killed her, then?"

"You aided and abetted, albeit unintentionally, but PC Garvey may still be alive if it wasn't for your stupidity." Bone stood. "Don't leave Kilwinnoch. You are free to go, for now."

Quinn stood, but he was so hunched and crushed by the weight of his guilt his height barely increased. He shuffled out.

Bone turned to Baxter. "Well?"

"He's a lowlife but not a murderer," Baxter said.

"And?"

"I need a fag," she replied.

Brody, the desk sergeant, stopped Bone on his way through the foyer. "Sir, there's a woman out there, and the press are going nuts."

Shouts and screams ensued. Bone peeked through the front door. An elderly woman, clearly in some distress, was being besieged by reporters, trying to push her way through to the forecourt and steps. Bone recognised her immediately. It was Margaret Edwards, the mother of Meiklejohn's first victim. He dashed out and shouldered his way through the pack as voices screamed questions at her. When he reached her, he put his arms around her shoulders.

"Come inside, Mrs Edwards," Bone shouted over the din.

"I've come to speak to you," Mrs Edwards puffed.

"Let the woman through!" Bone snapped at the pack. Shielding her from the assault, he guided her to the safety of the station.

Inside the foyer, the woman held a hand up to her chest, trying to catch her breath. "I needed to talk..." she wheezed.

"You need to come and sit down," Bone said. "Get Mrs Edwards a cup of tea, will you?" He winked at Brody and, taking the woman's arm, he helped her through the back and into the quiet of a waiting room. He helped her on to a chair and sat next to her.

"I'm so sorry about all that outside."

Mrs Edwards shook her head, her breathing still laboured. She reached for her handbag and tried to open the zip, but her hands shook too much.

"Let me. What do you want?" Bone took her bag.

"Inhaler," Mrs Edwards rasped.

Bone searched the bag and snatched out her medicine. She squirted the end two or three times, inhaling deeply, and within a few seconds her breathing stabilised. Brody appeared with a cup of tea and handed it to Bone.

"Are you okay? Would you like water instead?"

"No." She took a few more deep breaths. "I'm asthmatic. They were crushing me. I couldn't breathe." She shook her head, and after a few moments, her breathing finally steadied.

Bone frowned. "They have no respect."

"It reminded me of before." She removed a handkerchief from her bag and blew her nose. "I came because I have to know that Robert Meiklejohn is dead, and I need you to tell me."

"Yes, Mrs Edwards. He is dead."

"So why is all this starting again?"

"We don't know yet."

"It's just too hard to bear." Her eyes swelled with tears, and she sobbed.

"I'm so sorry," Bone moved closer. "Meiklejohn died in the explosion."

"Then why are the papers saying he's alive?"

"They make up these evil lies to sell their filthy rags. They don't think for one minute about how this affects you or your family."

She wiped her eyes and cheeks. "You are a kind man. I never blamed you like others did. You did your very best to catch him, and you suffered, too."

"Nothing like the pain you've gone through, Mrs Edwards." He offered her the tea.

She took a couple of sips and looked up at him.

"You know, I still talk to her, my Katie. We sit together in my conservatory and blether. I find it comforting."

"I'm glad," he said. "I'm sorry he wasn't tried and punished."

"Death was his punishment, it was the Lord's will," she said and took another sip.

"But what you need to do is stop reading the rubbish these papers print."

"I'm sorry to—"

"You don't have to apologise, Mrs Edwards, never," Bone cut in. "I'll always have time to speak to you. But maybe call ahead so you don't have to go through that again."

She tried to stand, and Bone took her arm.

"My daughter would be happy that you are in charge again," she said, shuffling to the door.

"Please be assured that we are working round the clock. We will stop this."

"Thank you, Inspector. I just needed to hear you say it."

"Let me arrange for a car to take you home."

"I walked here and I can walk back."

"I insist, and this way you don't have to face the hyenas."

"Then okay, yes. Thank you."

THIRTY-FIVE

When Bone returned to the incident room, Walker and Mullens were both back.

"s car has been found, burnt out on some waste ground on the outskirts of Livingston, and nothing else has turned up at the house," Walker said grimly.

"What about Scotsave, Mullens?" Bone asked.

"I spoke to the deputy manager, some wee spotty eight-year-old, who said that Will had taken everything they had recorded that night."

"Bollocks," Bone said.

"DCI Bone?"

They all turned at the voice at the door. It was DS Mohan from Campsie Fells Station.

"Hello, Sanjit," Bone said as Mohan approached. "I take it you've already heard about our colleague, DC Harper's abduction?"

"Aye, just awful. I've come over because I think I've found something that might help."

"What's that?" Bone asked.

"PC Ross, who was there that night, took a bunch of photographs of the group, and she sent them over to me. I've stuck them on this stick."

"This way." Bone led Mohan to the nearest desk and fired up the computer.

Walker joined them and gave Mohan a nod of hello.

"All yours," Bone said.

Mohan sat and plugged in the stick. He opened the folder, and the screen filled with multiple thumbnails. "So, she snapped away during the night."

He opened the gallery and flicked through the images of happy, smiley faces huddled round their table in the Fells, beaming at the camera. Then, as the images progressed, and the alcohol flowed and the table filled with glasses and bottles, the faces and smiles became a little blearier, the hugs a little tighter.

"It's these three here," Mohan said. "Bethany took these at a different angle, from farther back, and you can see she's captured some of the people at the bar."

Bone leaned in.

Mohan flicked forward. "In this one, PC Garvey can be seen leaning on the bar." He moved onto the next. "And then a moment later... Can you see that guy close by, and where his hand is?"

"Jesus, it's over her glass." Bone looked at Walker who had knelt by the desk.

"That's John Meiklejohn," Walker said. "I'd recognise that mangy coat anywhere."

"I knew it," Bone exclaimed. He stood. "That sick bastard is up to his neck in this." He grabbed his jacket. "Come on, Rhona."

He turned to Mohan who was leaning back on the chair, unsure of what was going on.

"Why don't you come as well, Sanjit, seeing as you're here? DS Mullens, meet DS Mohan. You two follow behind."

Mullens gave Mohan a nod, and they left together.

"Sheila, alert the firearms unit, but tell them to stay well clear. Will might be somewhere on that bastard's holding. Let's go," Bone said.

The cars pulled up at the end of the lane up to Meiklejohn's but and ben.

"Round the back," Bone whispered to Mullens who clambered awkwardly through the tumbledown fence and cut across a field, following the line of the hedge for cover. "You take the other side," Bone instructed Walker. "Mohan, you come with me."

Walker disappeared up the track, keeping her head low as Bone and Mohan approached the doorway. Bone peered through a gap in the board but couldn't see a thing.

"Let's move it slowly," he said.

Mohan helped him shift it sideways. They ventured inside cautiously, and Bone stopped.

"Listen," he whispered, but he couldn't hear anything other than their own breathing.

Bone inched in a little farther, with Mohan behind. As Bone's eyes adjusted, details in the room emerged from the gloom: the ancient inglenook on the far side, the table where Meiklejohn had sat tearing up strips of paper for his fire, now vacant. The room was empty. He carried on to the back room, where Meiklejohn had created his macabre shrine to his son.

"What is this?" Mohan whispered.

"Insanity," Bone replied.

There was a sudden loud clatter directly behind them. They spun round. A figure lunged towards them in the dark. Mohan cut in front of Bone to block the assailant.

"Whoa, it's me," Mullens' familiar baritone rumbled out of the darkness.

"Jesus, Mark." Bone recoiled.

"There's nobody out the back," Mullens rasped his version of a whisper.

Just then, Walker's familiar whistle sounded. Bone dashed through the house and out the front. She whistled again. It was coming from a near-derelict hay store at the far side of the holding. Walker stood in the entrance when they reached her. She nodded inside, and they followed her in. At the back of the barn, Meiklejohn's limp body swung gently from one of the rusty iron rafters. One of his shoes dangled from the end of his foot, threatening to fall, his snapped neck leaning at a near ninety-degree angle to his shoulders.

"Suicide?" Walker asked sceptically.

"My arse," Bone replied. "Somebody got to him before we did."

"Who?"

"Well, it's not that wee no-hope labourer, that's for sure." Bone shrugged.

"Do you think it's wise to go after McLean?" Walker continued. "Is he capable of this?"

They all stared back at the body creaking back and forth.

"Chief Officer Ross McLean? He's your main suspect?" Mohan said.

Bone nodded. "Our priority is to find Will alive. Let's go."

"Shouldn't we cut him down or something?" Mohan asked.

Bone shook his head. "He's not going anywhere. Leave it for SOC. Come on."

"I'll call it in, sir," Walker said. "And no sign of DC Harper."

"Hoy!" Mullen's booming voice called from across the yard.

"What is it?" Bone asked, approaching his colleague.

Mullens hovered over the charred remains of Meiklejohn's bonfire.

"When I was out here the other day, I saw him burning a whole load of crap on this fire," he said, poking at the ashes with his boot. He knelt. "See this?" He picked out a half-incinerated bundle of papers and placed it on the ground. "It looks like a bunch of letters." He carefully leafed through the charred remains.

"They're from his son." Bone immediately recognised Peek-a-boo's scratchy handwriting.

"This one's in reasonable nick." Mullens eased the paper out from the centre of the burnt clump. "Shit!" he exclaimed. "This bit here is all about Peek-a-boo's first kill." He turned it over and continued to read. "Jesus, this is graphic."

"So it would appear Peek-a-boo was keeping his dad updated on his killing spree," Bone replied.

"And he did nothing to stop him. Evil bastards, the two of them." Mullens scowled.

"How did we miss that?" Bone said. "We interviewed John Meiklejohn countless times during the first investigation."

"The auld prick was a good liar, like his son," Mullens said. "So was this blackmail as well?"

"Looks like it," Bone said. "He was clearly in a hurry to get rid."

"SOC will be here in ten minutes, sir," Walker said.

Bone stepped back "Okay, you and Sanjit wait for forensics, and fill them in. Come on, Mark. This place is making me feel ill."

"Sir, I have a confession to make," Mullens said, catching up with Bone on the way back to the car.

"What have you done now?"

"You know how you told me to keep tabs on his movements. Well, I kind of left early."

"How so?"

"My dad rang me, he said it was an emergency, so I left before I found out what Meiklejohn was burning. And now he's in there chilling with the bats. Maybe if I'd stuck around, I might have stopped him or seen who did it."

"Don't worry about it, Mark, he's only been up there a few hours, long after you were here," Bone said. "But you need to seriously think about getting your dad into care."

"Tell me about it," Mullens replied, and glancing at Bone, he added, "Thank you, sir."

THIRTY-SIX

A uniformed officer stood to attention outside the incident room. Bone approached and he stepped forward.

"Sir, the DSU would like to see you," the officer said sheepishly.

"What is this?"

"Please, sir." The PC gestured for Bone to follow.

"So he's sending errand boys now? Jesus," Bone grumbled, but he followed anyway.

The incident room door opened, and Walker stepped out into the corridor. "What's going on?" she called, looking bemused.

Bone shrugged and continued to follow and the PC walked past Gallacher's office. Bone stopped and raised his hand.

"This is his office."

"Follow me, sir, please," the uniform insisted.

He took Bone downstairs and stopped outside the first interview room.

"In here?" Bone asked.

The PC knocked on the door and opened it. "DCI Bone is here, sir," he said briskly and ushered Bone in.

"What the hell is going on?" Bone started.

Gallacher was dressed in full uniform, including his cap, perched behind an interview table, flanked on one side by a familiar face from Bone's past — DCS Barnes from Edinburgh Central, his Rottweiler features glaring at Bone. On Gallacher's other side sat Special Investigator Tennyson, who smiled as he approached. A figure also sat at the back, behind the welcoming party.

"Afternoon, Detective, long time no see," Bone said to the unflinching Rottweiler. He glanced over at Gallacher. "What's with the welcome party?"

"Sit down, please, DCI Bone," Barnes ordered, his growl indicating that something horrendous was about to happen.

Bone complied and sat opposite.

"I see our friend Mr McLean's been busy then." Bone smirked. He spotted a VHS video tape resting on the table next to the audio recorder.

"For the record, I'm Assistant Chief Constable Frank Barnes from Edinburgh Central."

"For the record? Am I under arrest?"

"Also in attendance, Detective Superintendent Roy Gallacher, Special Investigator Sarah Tennyson, and Welfare Officer, David Ross."

"What is this?" Bone growled.

"This morning, DSU Gallacher received this video tape in the post." Barnes picked it up.

"Cat got your tongue, sir?" Bone said sarcastically.

Gallacher frowned.

"Fearing this could be another abduction, Detective Superintendent Gallacher asked IT to convert the content to mp4," Barnes continued.

"Is this story serialised or a one-off movie?" Bone's patience was all but broken.

Barnes opened up the laptop and pushed it against the wall so Bone could see the screen. "The VCR contained CCTV footage of what we believe is PC Garvey in the Scotsave car park on the night of her abduction."

"That tape was stolen from Will's house, sir." Bone addressed his comment to Gallacher.

Barnes ignored him and pressed play. The screen burst into life with an image of a deserted car park.

"And?" Bone said impatiently.

The video continued to play. The blur of a car shot past the entrance at speed. Barnes hit the pause button.

"Not exactly Oscar-winning. What is your point?" Bone scowled.

He glanced over at Tennyson who scribbled notes on a reporter's pad.

"IT isolated the passing vehicle captured in the footage. They cleaned up the image and improved clarity and definition as much as technology would allow." Barnes pressed play again, but this time in frame-by-frame slow motion. The front of the car appeared, and when the whole vehicle was captured on the screen, the footage froze. "What make and model of car would you say that is, DCI Bone?"

Bone's mouth fell open. "I don't understand," he said, lost for words.

"Is that your car, DCI Bone?"

"It's not possible."

"How many Saab vehicles of that age are there in Kilwinnoch?" Barnes persisted.

"This is wrong."

"So you agree that the car in the recording is yours?"

"I don't…"

"You may also remember that a few fibres were collected from the deceased during the forensic inspection."

"Here we go…" Bone shook his head.

"Results have so far identified a manufacturer match."

"Let me guess, a Saab ninety-six, circa nineteen seventy-four?" Bone groaned.

"That is still to be determined. We will need to impound your car."

"Oh, come on!" Bone stood.

The PC over by the door approached.

"I bet you're loving this," Bone snapped at Tennyson.

She glanced up, smiled, and stopped writing. As she placed her pen down, her hand turned out momentarily, and Bone caught a fleeting glimpse of a black mark on the underside of her fingers.

"Sit down, DCI Bone," Barnes ordered.

Bone reluctantly lowered himself back down.

"Where were you on the evening of the twenty-eighth of September, the night PC Garvey was abducted and murdered?"

"I'm a suspect now?"

"You have admitted that the car in the CCTV footage is yours," Barnes replied.

"So — I'm the killer. I murdered PC Garvey and now my colleague, who I admire greatly despite his unhealthy obsession with *Star Wars*, I'm prepping him for a live broadcast public embalming session. Have I missed anything?"

"Where were you, Inspector?" Barnes repeated.

"At home — I can't believe I'm going along with this circus. I was in bed, enjoying my sick leave, and now wish I'd told you to fuck off, Detective Superintendent Gallacher, *sir*."

He scowled at his boss.

"Watch your language, DCI Bone," Gallacher warned.

"And can anyone corroborate your story?" Barnes carried on.

"It's not a story, Columbo." Bone sighed.

"When you returned to active duty, would you say you were ready?"

Bone threw up his hands. "Oh, stop. Just do what you have to do."

"The Deputy Chief Constable of Scotland hereby orders your suspension from active duty from henceforth, pending further investigation." Barnes picked an A4 envelope that rested by his notes and handed it to Bone. "You are not under arrest at this stage, but we will need to speak to you again, so please do not leave Kilwinnoch."

"This is all McLean. He's told you to do this, hasn't he?"

"SOP, Inspector, you know that," Barnes replied. "Welfare Officer Ross is here to offer his support and advice if you wish."

"And you have nothing to say, DSU Gallacher?" Bone looked over at his boss.

"Out of my hands," Gallacher replied, avoiding eye contact.

"Come on, Roy, I'm being framed. You know that. Whoever is doing this — maybe that bastard McLean — has somehow got a hold of my car."

"How is that possible?" Tennyson suddenly spoke.

Barnes frowned at her.

"What was that?" Bone responded.

She sat back.

Barnes held up a pen. "I'll need you to sign both copies."

Bone tore open the envelope, removed the letter, and scrawled across the front.

"And the copy, for your own records," Barnes insisted.

"Farce," Bone snarled, signed again, and dropped it onto the table.

"That's for you."

"Frame it and post it to me."

"And we'll need your warrant card," Barnes continued, unfazed.

Bone removed his lanyard and threw it with such force that it skittered across the table and landed in Gallacher's lap. He spun round, and the PC who still hovered close by stepped back slightly.

"Am I free to leave, or are we pressing charges?"

"You're free to go for now, but as I said, you'll be called in again shortly," Barnes said. "I suggest you take full advantage of the support offered by welfare, and I strongly recommend you contact a solicitor."

"I might ask Advocate McLean to represent me," Bone sneered and tried to leave, but the PC stopped him at the door.

"PC Stevenson will escort you out of the station," Barnes called over.

"So I can't even pick up my belongings from the incident room?"

"I'm sure one of your colleagues would be willing drop them round for you." Barnes smiled, clearly enjoying his moment of victory.

Bone opened his mouth to unleash his rage but then changed his mind and followed the PC out.

Halfway down the corridor, Bone stopped. "I'd rather go out the back."

They went back and exited through a side door, and then out across the rear car park. At the gate, the PC turned.

"Sir, for what it's worth, everybody here is right behind you."

Bone nodded, and the PC opened the gate. As Bone crossed the street, the SOC team were already busy loading his car up onto a trailer. McKinnon, the *Chronicle's* journalist, appeared from nowhere.

"Early bath, Inspector?" McKinnon said with an insincere smile.

"Fuck off, weasel." Bone pushed past him.

"You clearly escaped arrest, so was it a caution or full-on suspension?"

Bone snapped, grabbed McKinnon by the throat, and rammed him up against a wall. "Who's feeding you this information?"

"A journalist never reveals his sources, Inspector," the journalist wheezed.

Bone tightened his grip around the man's neck. "I could have you arrested as a suspect."

McKinnon shook his head, his face becoming more and more flushed as he struggled to breathe. Reluctantly, Bone released his grip.

"I could add assault to your woes," McKinnon spluttered, clutching at his throat.

"Look. We've known each other a long time and we both know it's not exactly Thelma and Louise between us, but we're trying to catch a cop killer here, and I need your help." Bone decided to take a more reasoned approach. "Come on, Colin, help me out. Who's feeding you this information?"

"Like I said, I'm not at liberty to inform you of that, but let's just say it's someone very close to the case."

"Who, for fuck sake?" Bone snapped back, on the verge of grabbing his neck again, and this time not stopping until his rodent features ceased twitching.

"Very close," McKinnon added.

REID

Bone raised his fist to punch the journalist, who shrank back against the wall, but then Bone stepped away.

"Get out of my sight, you're contaminating my air."

McKinnon scurried off, and when he was a safe distance, he took a couple of snaps of Bone's car being towed away. Bone started to chase him, and he spun round and ran for it.

On the way back to his flat, Bone's phone rang.

"You've heard then?" Bone said, answering.

"What the hell is going on?" Walker's voice was shaking. "DCS Barnes has just turned up. He says you've been suspended and he's now in charge of the investigation."

"Listen, never mind that," Bone replied.

"Never mind that? Jesus, Duncan. Barnes has put your bloody photo up on the incident board."

"I need Baxter to pull up the records of Special Investigator Tennyson."

"Why?"

"Everything she can find," Bone continued. "Tell her to go back as far as she can, work, personal stuff — all of it, okay?"

"Okay, but you still haven't explained why?"

"Remember the bitumen on Meiklejohn's makeshift door?"

"Remember it? I can't get rid of the bloody stuff from my hands."

"Neither can Tennyson. I think she paid him a visit. Ask Baxter to send it all over to me, and when she's done that, I'm going to need your help."

"Your place?" Walker replied without hesitation.

"In an hour." Bone paused. "Unless you're worried about associating with a suspect."

"Bollocks to that," Walker retorted.

***

Bone legged it over to Alice's house and thumped the door with his fist. "Come on, come on," he cried, and rapped it again.

Alice finally answered the door with her usual flustered expression. "It's not a good time, Duncan."

"Aw, thank Christ, Alice. Listen to me. I need you to do something for me."

"What?" she said, her tone already veering towards a rebuttal.

"Take Michael up to your mum's for a couple of days."

"Are you having a laugh?" Alice shrugged. "I mean, what?"

"I'm serious," Bone urged.

"But Michael is in school, and I've got a load of stuff to do. We can't just drop it all on your say-so. I mean, why? What's going on?"

"You're going to have to trust me. Please, just take Michael. It's only for a few days, and then things should be fine."

"Is it to do with this case, in the papers?"

"Things are getting complicated."

"Jesus, Duncan. Things are *always* complicated with you. What possessed you to get involved in this of all cases?"

"There's no time for this now. Please, you know I wouldn't ask. Just do this for me."

"It's really difficult. Me and Mum don't exactly get on."

"Michael loves it up there, with the hens and sheep, and they'll be lambing now, too," he said, clutching desperately at straws. "Please, Alice."

"I'll ring Mum and see what she says, but if she gives me a hard time then…"

"Thank you!" Bone exclaimed with relief. "Shall I go and get Michael?"

"You mean right now?"

"Yes."

"Bloody hell." She sighed. "Okay, but I'll get him, you go back to your complication." She could see the panic spiralling in Bone's eyes, and her mind was clearly now almost entirely on her son's safety.

Bone was about to thank her again, but Alice had already shut the door.

THIRTY-SEVEN

Bone's laptop pinged frantically as Baxter sent through files and documents on Tennyson. As Bone had first surmised, she was public school educated, but instead of the usual trajectory to Oxbridge, she'd chosen a career in the army instead, training as an officer in the rifle regiment. He clicked a couple of further links that took him to an image of her arm in arm with a group of soldiers by a field tent, in some desert location. The caption below it read 'Afghanistan 2004'.

A couple more pings, and more documents landed. He couldn't find out if Tennyson had seen active combat, but another record caught his eye. She'd taken additional training as a bomb disposal officer and returned to the Middle East in 2008 to help clear landmines. Then, in 2009, her army record stopped. She'd discharged herself. He searched around the period, but there was no indication why. However, in the following year, she'd enrolled on a criminal psychology degree course at the University of Glasgow. Following that, she'd worked for the

Scottish prison service, which led to her promotion as a Special Police Investigator.

Bone picked up the phone and called Baxter.

"Sir, I'm so sorry about what's happened," Baxter said as soon as she heard Bone's voice.

"Can you look for any details around Tennyson's time as a student, and then when she worked as a criminal psychologist with SPS and then with us?" Bone asked.

"Yes, sir, I'll see what I can find." She hung up.

Bone returned to the screen, but the doorbell interrupted him.

"Sir, I think I've found something." Walker stood in the doorway, looking flustered.

Bone let her in.

"Where's your laptop?" She marched down his hallway.

"In here." Bone took her over to the dining table in the living room. "What is it?" He opened the lid, and the screen woke up.

Walker inserted a USB. "Something was bugging me about the video of Will so I asked IT to run it through the same app that Will has been using, to help pick out any detail that we might be missing."

"So you're going to make me watch this horror show again?"

"Sorry, but it's only a short extract, and you'll see why I need you to see it."

Walker cued the file, and the recording played in slow motion, now zoomed in on Will's exposed left eye, his lid opening and closing repeatedly. After twenty or so seconds the video stopped, and Walker glanced up.

"Did you see it?" she asked.

"What?" Bone was still confused.

"I think that's Morse code. Watch again."

"And you know this how?"

"Venture Scout, remember?" she replied, and hit the replay.

"That's B-O-I-L-E-R," Walker said as the sequence played through again.

"Huh?" Bone asked in bewilderment.

She played it one more time, pointing at the screen each time Harper blinked. "B-O-I-L-E-R, I'm sure of it."

"What does he mean?" Bone squinted at her.

"Maybe something to do with his boiler, back at his house?"

"Shit. Genius. Let's go."

THIRTY-EIGHT

Bone asked Walker to pull up at the end of Harper's road.

"I'd better wait here. The PCs won't let me through, and if they see you with me, you'll be in deep shit."

"Wait here a minute," she said and climbed out.

Bone watched her approach the PC who was stationed by Harper's front gate. After a few words, the PC nodded, then ran off up the street to the end and disappeared round the corner. Walker ran back to the car.

"We've only got a few minutes. I've told him to go and check the lane at the back from end to end as I just saw what looked like a couple of neds trying to break into number one." She pointed to the first house at the farthest end of the street and smiled.

Bone jumped out. Dashing to Harper's gate, he and Walker ducked under the police tape and ran up to the door.

"How do we get in?" Bone asked.

Walker produced a set of keys. "Spare set in Will's office drawer."

She opened the door, and they went inside.

In the kitchen, Bone checked a few cupboards. "Where's the bloody boiler?" he said, opening and closing a few more.

They moved back into the hall, and Walker spotted the airing cupboard and opened up.

"Said boiler," she said.

Bone scanned the front of the box, then bent over and checked the myriad pipes and valves underneath. He ran his hand round the side and then squeezed his fingers into a narrow gap between the unit and the wall. His nail scraped against something hard that didn't sound like a pipe. He gave it a nudge, and a VHS tape tumbled out the other side, landing on the floor at Walker's feet.

"The Scotsave tape?" Bone picked it up.

"I thought that had been sent to Gallacher?" Walker replied.

"Will has a machine here, doesn't he?" Bone said. He dashed back through to the living room. The video recorder was still resting on the coffee table where Harper had left it. "I'll plug it into the TV." He checked the back of the VCR, but the cables were missing. "Bugger."

Walker spotted the box resting on the wall by the window. Picking it up, she turned it upside down, and a mess of cables spilled out. She brought them over, and after a fight to disentangle them from each other, Bone located the TV connector, plugged it all in, and switched on all the equipment.

"The perks of being into retro." He inserted the tape in the machine, and after a couple of false starts, he got the VCR and TV talking to each other. He pressed play, but nothing happened. "Buggeration."

"Wait." Walker reached round the back of the machine and swapped some cables round. "Try again."

The TV screen flickered, and the video rolled.

"Scotsave must have two CCTV cameras in the car park," Bone said. But his words were cut short when the car stopped by the gate and the driver glanced up at the screen. He hit rewind and played it again. He looked back at Walker. "It's fucking Tennyson."

"It would appear so," Walker replied.

"So that's why Peek-a-boo kept saying, 'my old friend,'" Bone muttered.

"What?" Walker asked.

But Bone was already on his mobile. "Roy, it's me," he said the second Gallacher answered.

"Duncan, the whole thing is out of my hands."

"Listen," Bone cut him off. "Is Tennyson still there?"

"What?"

"The Special Investigator, is she still in the station?"

"Duncan, you are suspended and under investigation. I shouldn't even be speaking to you right now."

"Just tell me," Bone urged.

"I think so, yes. I saw her in the corridor ten minutes or so ago. What's going on?"

"She abducted PC Garvey and has probably got Harper."

"Jesus Christ, Duncan. You really have lost it."

"I'm at DC Harper's house. I've recovered CCTV footage of Tennyson driving my car and picking up Garvey. Irrefutable evidence."

"You shouldn't be in his house. Have you broken in?"

"Yes, I broke in. I'm on my own."

Walker snatched the phone from Bone's hands.

"Sir, I'm here with DCI Bone. I've seen the footage, too. It's true. Tennyson is our target." Silence. "Sir?"

"What do you want me to do?" Gallacher said finally.

Bone grabbed his phone back. "Keep her there as long as you can."

"What are you going to do?"

"We're going to find Will."

"This is one fucked-up case," Gallacher said. "You need to stay out of it, Duncan, and let DI Walker—"

But Bone cut him off and called Baxter. "I need Tennyson's address."

Moments later, Baxter was back. "Twenty-three Cedric Road, Mossilpark."

"Tell Mark to follow Tennyson if she leaves the station." Bone hung up. "How long will it take to get to Mossilpark?"

"Me or you driving?" Walker replied. "Twenty-five minutes, give or take."

"Let's go."

As they left the house, the flustered and sweaty PC arrived back at the front entrance.

"No sign of…" He stopped as Walker and Bone pushed past. "…intruders," he wheezed and collapsed against the wall, exhausted.

Fifteen minutes later, and five minutes faster than *Top Gear's* Stig could have managed it, Walker swung the car into Cedric Road and pulled up.

"Twenty-three is this way," Walker said, scanning the numbers on the terrace.

"Come on," Bone said.

They scrambled out of the car and marched up the street.

Luckily, number twenty-three was an end terrace property. They dashed round the side and, finding a gate in the high fence, Bone tried the handle. It was locked. He put his shoulder to it, but it refused to budge.

"Shimmy?" Walker crouched with her hands cupped.

Bone lifted his foot, and Walker practically threw him up and over. He jumped down into the modest courtyard and opened the gate to let Walker in. Then he tried the door.

"Sir," Walker whispered and pointed to the sash window. She thumped the frame twice, and the window sprang open.

"How the hell do you do that?" Bone shrugged and climbed in. The kitchen was gloomy and claustrophobically small. "You search down here, I'll check upstairs."

He leapt up the narrow staircase and tried the first door. A bathroom. He quickly scanned the space and then carried on. A single bedroom next. Its spartan interior indicated an unused spare room. He tried the third. It was Tennyson's bedroom. He edged in to examine the dressing table, a cluttered mess of cosmetics, toiletries, and other paraphernalia. He pulled at a drawer beneath, which was crammed with knickers and bras. Opening a narrow wardrobe in the corner, he fished around in some of the jacket and coat pockets, but aside from a half-eaten packet of Polos and some used handkerchiefs, there was nothing of any use. He moved over to the side table by her bed. A novel rested on the top. He glanced at the title. *Bravo Two Zero* by Andy McNab.

"That's about right," he mumbled.

On a shelf below, a metal in-tray heaped with papers. Bone knelt and flicked through the pile but then spotted a key tucked between two envelopes. He held it under the lamp for a closer look. It was the key for his Saab, or at least a pristine replica of it, with the same distinctive seventies logo on the finger bow.

He was about to make a quick exit when he spotted a slip of paper lying on the floor beneath the bed. Kneeling, he reached underneath. It was a bookmark, and on the back there was a mobile number, hand-scribbled along its length. Fumbling with his phone again, he quickly punched in the digits. The call clicked and rang, and almost immediately, someone answered.

"Who is this?" Bone asked.

"Depot Storage Units, sir. How can I help?"

As soon as Bone hung up, it rang again. "Bugger," he muttered, stabbing at the front. "Yes?"

"Tennyson left twenty minutes ago. I thought she was still in her office, sorry," Gallacher said.

"Depot Storage Units on the old Fells Road. Alert the tactical unit, but don't send them in yet. The last thing we need is Tennyson getting spooked. I'll ring you back."

"Bone...Bone!" Gallacher hollered down the phone.

But Bone hung up. He dived downstairs.

"I think I might have just found Will," he said to Walker breathlessly.

THIRTY-NINE

The storage units were located on the former papermill site out on the old main road between Kilwinnoch and Campsie Fells. The lock-ups varied in size, but most were large enough to store the possessions of the average house or a couple of cars. The company hadn't bothered to do much with the old paper mill. Instead, they had installed the metal containers around and between the buildings. As Walker approached the turning into the lane, she slowed.

"Gallacher's bound to have called in the tactical unit," she said. "And if they are there, they won't let you through." She stopped, then reversed down the road and pulled into a lay-by.

"I know another way in," she said.

Bone followed her out of the car. They ran back up the road, and Walker climbed over a stile and into a field, the half-moon in an unusually clear sky providing sufficient light to see the track.

"This way," she said, and she dropped down a bank to the side of a fast-flowing burn.

Bone scrambled down after her.

"Are you sure this is right?" he asked, stumbling over some rocks.

"This runs right into the middle of the mill." She leapt expertly from one boulder to the next.

A couple more slips and Bone was in the burn up to his knees, but he carried on. A few minutes later, they reached the first outbuilding. The river narrowed, making it marginally easier to negotiate. They followed it under a bridge, Bone clinging to the side as the water lapped around his ankles. On the other side, the main site was now in view, Vast steel units were bolted on to existing buildings. Keeping low, they climbed up the bank and into the yard, using a line of oil barrels as cover.

"He could be in any of these," Bone whispered.

Walker pointed across the yard to a faint light just visible through a windowless gap in one of the old buildings. They weaved around the edge of the yard, tucking in close to the buildings. When they got to the target building, Bone gestured to Walker to go round the side, and he approached the front cautiously. Crouching, he poked his head up and peered through the window. The light was coming from farther in.

He searched the front but couldn't see a door, so he slid over and through the hole in the wall, then rolled onto the stone floor inside. He turned at a loud click to his left. Someone moved in the darkness. He pushed farther into the wall and held his breath. The shadow shifted sideways and then disappeared. He leaned forward for a better view, but his foot caught the wall, and a lump of plaster tumbled off, smacking the floor with a loud *whack*.

Bone jumped up, anticipating an attack from the shadows, but all was silent. He continued along the wall, heading for the pinhole of light up ahead, but as he ventured deeper into the building, the darkness intensified. He stumbled on something at his feet, stopped, listened, and continued. Approaching the source of the light, it suddenly extinguished, and pitch-blackness engulfed him. He was now completely blind but he stumbled on, using the wall as a guide. Four or five steps, and his hand made contact with cold, smooth metal. The side of a unit or maybe a door. He ran his palm up and down the surface, searching for a handle, and with a soft creak, it swung open. He stepped through and, reaching out, he peered into the impenetrable darkness.

Suddenly, someone grabbed his arm, yanking him forward and down towards the floor. Instinctively, he twisted and rolled over, releasing the lock. He leaped up and backwards, but was struck from the side, the force of the blow knocking him to the floor again. Jumping onto his haunches, he charged into the dark in full scrum position and slammed into a body. They tumbled in a tangle together, fists and feet flailing. Bone grabbed a handful of fabric or hair, and with his free fist, he pummelled the assailant's body, his knuckles finally connecting with skin and hard bone. The attacker wrapped an arm around Bone's neck and twisted his neck like a cork in a bottle. Bone tried to squirm out of the hold, but it was too tight, and he gagged for air.

He scratched at the ground and his finger brushed against something hard. A brick. He threw his weight sideways to reach the weapon. He snatched it up and smashed it into the side of the attacker's skull. The attacker's arms dropped, and Bone scrambled out from under the motionless body. Gasping for air, he fumbled for his phone and turned on the torch, aiming the beam onto the floor where his assailant was lying. But there was nobody there.

"Fuck!" Another crack behind him, and he shot round, his fists raised.

"Sir, it's me!" Walker emerged from the darkness.

"Jesus!" Bone said.

"What was all the noise?"

"Shh," Bone hissed. He fired the beam back into the room.

Walker shifted forward, following the beam, searching the space.

"She's in here somewhere," Bone whispered.

Spinning round, he shone the beam ahead and snatched a glimpse of a chair. Walker followed him cautiously. Bone swung the beam, and the light landed on Harper's half-naked body.

Bone rushed over. "Will?" he said, handing Walker the torch. "Will!" He shook him but Harper didn't respond. Bone checked the pulse in his neck.

"He's still alive. Just!" he said.

"Look at that." Walker shone the beam on the bottle on the floor, now over half full with Harper's drained blood.

A door slammed at the far side of the room. Bone jumped up.

"Call an ambulance," he ordered and ran across the room out into the yard.

The moonlight illuminated a figure running across it.

"Tennyson!" Bone shouted.

The figure stopped for a second and then carried on, disappearing behind one of the lock-ups. Bone gave chase. But when he reached the lock-up there was no sign. He did a quick three-sixty, but the person was gone. He continued to the end of the building, to the rear fence. He rattled the wire and spotted a hole to his left, cut wide enough to crawl through. Pushing through, he scrambled to his feet and ran down a track by the side of a field. When he reached the end, he jumped the wall back onto the road. A set of headlights exploded in his face, and he leapt sideways onto the bank as a car narrowly missed him and sped past.

He sprinted up the road to where they'd left the pool car and stopped. "No keys!" He fumbled for his phone. "No phone. Fuuuck!"

Just then, another set of headlights appeared over the brow of the hill. A patrol car. He ran out onto the road and into its path.

The driver hit the brakes, and it screeched to a halt about three feet from him. An officer jumped out.

"I need your car!" Bone cried.

"Who are you?" the officer said incredulously.

"DCI Bone. I need to follow the car that just passed you."

"DCI Bone, aren't you suspended?"

"Well, bloody arrest me then, but just turn your car around and follow the fucking cop killer."

"Aye, sir," the officer said.

They ran back to the car. With a screeching U-turn, the officer accelerated back up the lane.

"Can you see it?" Bone said from the front passenger seat, scouring the darkness for signs of headlights.

"There." The young officer in the back pointed at the moving beams on the hillside.

"He's taken the Rest Road, up over the top," the driver said.

"Shall we request backup?" the PC in the back asked.

"Yes, the suspect is armed and very dangerous," Bone said. "But tell them to keep their distance. We don't want a bloodbath." He leaned over and squinted at the speedometer. "Does this thing go any faster?"

"Oh aye." The officer grinned, and crunching the gears, he put his foot down. At the turning onto Rest Road, he barely slowed, and the squad car screamed round the corner. "This road is bastard windy. Better tighten your belts."

The crimson glow of Tennyson's rear lights were now visible ahead. They were gaining on her. The car wound towards the summit, the road narrowing with a sheer drop on their nearside, but the driver handled tight turns at breakneck speed with trained assurance, and they soon reached the top where the road widened out again. The officer in the back mumbled something incoherent.

"What was that, Jim?" the driver asked.

"I said I think I'm..." The officer quickly wound down his window, stuck his head out, and retched over the side of the door, the spew flailing out behind like a red arrow display of diced carrots.

"Jesus Christ," the driver complained. "You're cleaning that up when we get back to the station."

The ashen-faced officer wiped his mouth. "I'm no used to it in the back."

"Got you, you bastard," Bone exclaimed, spotting Tennyson's rear lights again, up ahead and closer still.

But then her car took a sudden right and disappeared down a track.

"Where the hell is she going?" Bone said.

"It's a cut through to the main road, hold on," the driver said, and the car swerved into the lane, bouncing and rattling violently in potholes and foot-deep tractor marks.

"Oh, for God's sake," Officer Jim grumbled and then gagged again.

When they finally reached the end of the track and the main road, they stopped.

"Which way?" the driver said.

Bone looked left and right. "There!" A flicker of light bounced off a cluster of pine trees.

They crossed over the main road and headed down another narrow lane.

"Where does this go?" Bone asked, the high hedges zooming past on either side.

"Out towards Carronhead, and then on to Stirling," the driver replied, wrestling with the steering wheel as the car careered down the track.

"Carronhead?" Bone repeated.

"Aye."

"Oh shit."

"What?" The driver glanced over and the side of the car brushed against an overhanging branch, whacking Bone's window.

"That's where my wife is."

The driver pushed the accelerator harder to the floor, and on the next turn, the ominous blood-red glow of Tennyson's rear lights reappeared ahead.

On the outskirts of Carronhead, a posse of flashing blue lights appeared behind them.

"Is that their idea of a low profile?" Bone grumbled.

Tennyson's car took another sharp right and veered off into a housing estate. The squad car followed, weaving past row upon row of shoebox sheltered housing rammed together in bland uniformity. The driver suddenly veered left.

"What are you doing? You'll lose her!"

"Shortcut," the driver replied and then took an immediate left again, roaring down another identical street. At the junction, he rammed on the brakes. "Wait for it," he said, and moments later, Tennyson's car sped past, and he tore after it with tyres screeching.

"Good call," the PC in the back said, the colour returning to his face.

Tennyson's car raced on through the village centre and then out the other side.

Bone prayed she would continue on, but to his horror, she turned into the lane leading to Alice's mother's holding.

"That's where she's going — go faster!" Bone said.

The rear headlights disappeared round yet another sharp corner, and when the squad car reached the bend, Tennyson's car had disappeared. The driver hit the brakes.

"Don't stop!" Bone yelled.

"We've lost it." The driver pummelled the steering wheel.

"Keep going!"

He slammed into second and roared off again.

"Take the next left," Bone said.

The driver spun the car round and onto another track.

"See the house up there, with the lights on?"

The PC nodded and carried on, arriving at the farm gate. Tennyson's car sat just beyond, the driver's door open and the engine still running.

Bone looked round the car. "Do you carry any weapons?"

"Just the usual," the driver said. "Have you brought the pepper spray?" he asked his colleague in the back.

"Sorry," the young PC said. "There could be a taser in the boot, I'll go and check." He started to climb out of the car.

"No time, give me your baton," Bone said to the driver.

The officer reached into the side pocket in the door and fished out the weapon. Bone snatched it from his hand, and they all jumped out. The two officers buttoned their vests and tooled up.

The driver dashed round to the boot and removed a stab vest. "Here, put this on, sir."

"You two, go round either side of the house. Be careful." Bone zipped up the vest.

Against all professional instincts, he ran up to the farmhouse and hammered frantically on the front door.

"Alice!" he hollered, and then listened. Nothing. He yanked the handle. But it was locked, and peering in through the nearest window, he couldn't see anything beyond the frame. He was about to dash round the side when the front door sprang open. Bone raised his truncheon in readiness to strike... and then Ruth, Alice's mother, stepped back in surprise.

"Duncan, what are you doing?"

"Oh, thank God," Bone said with relief.

Michael appeared behind the woman. "Dad!" he cried, and pushing past his gran, leapt into his father's arms.

"Where's Alice?" Bone peered down the hall.

"She's over in the office helping me sort out my accounts," Ruth replied. "She's been in there for hours. I hope I've not messed up again." Then she spotted the convoy of flashing police cars heading up the lane to the house. "What's going on, Duncan?" she asked anxiously.

"Take Michael, get inside, lock the doors, and stay away from the windows." He handed his wriggling son back to Ruth. "Now!" he shouted.

She slammed the door. As he ran round the side, a whistle pierced the air, and he headed towards the old stables, now converted to Ruth's makeshift office. He ducked along the side of the trailer and made a run for the building. He slid along the wall and peeked through the half-open stable door. The office was deserted. He returned to the door, tried the handle and gave the door a gentle nudge. Raising his truncheon, he was about to charge in when a burning pain shot across his skull, and before he could scream, he blacked out.

Bone opened his eyes, the glare of the office's fluorescent light stabbing at his skull like a cobra bite. His mind was groggy and unresponsive, and it took him a few seconds to work out where he was. He looked down. He was propped up in a chair, his wrists bound, and the police vest he'd put on at the car was splattered in blood. His eyes blurred, and he almost passed out. He shook his head and brought himself back. The vest was different. It was wrapped in a tangle of wires, with a row of rod-like objects stretched across his chest. *A suicide vest. Fuck!*

"Peek-a-boo!"

He spun his head at the whisper in his ear. Tennyson appeared from the darkness and stood over him.

"Well, don't you look handsome?" she hissed, her black combat jacket muddied and torn at the shoulder.

"Jennifer Bailey," Bone slurred.

"Ah, you're good. I'll give you that, Inspector," Tennyson sneered.

"Where's my wife? What have you done with her?" Bone tugged at the ties but they were too tight.

"She's having a wee lie down. Terribly tiring being married to you, I hear."

Bone spotted a fist-sized detonator switch in her hand.

"I hated the Baileys, the foster family from hell," she continued. "Tennyson suits me, though, don't you think? I mean, it's clever, isn't it? I would never make that up, it's too obvious." She turned the device so Bone could see a white button protruding from the side. "They were very good to me." She eyeballed him. "Enjoying your trip down Memory Lane?" Her sneer returned.

"None of this is going to bring him back," Bone croaked.

"You took him from me."

"He did that to himself."

"You destroyed everything we had, and now I'm going to do the same to you and Sleeping Beauty in there." She nodded to the back room. Her thumb hovered over the button.

"Eye for an eye, is that it?" Bone cut in. "How pathetic. He was a real-deal serial killer. What are you? Some sad, obsessed fan? He's laughing at you now. You know that, don't you?"

"Shut up!" She thrust her arm out, threatening to press the button again.

"One thing I don't get. Why kill that poor office clerk for those files? I mean, come on. Your psycho boyfriend wouldn't have been so stupid."

"I gave this to him, and you stole it from me." She pulled a neck chain out from under her jacket. "St. Christopher," she said, stroking a buckled and blackened pendant dangling from the end. "He called it his lucky talisman."

"Well, that clearly worked. And Sam Tozier died for that?"

"He was a vessel."

"He's a dead vessel, and another destroyed family."

"He loved me," Tennyson said. "You have no idea."

"He loved me," Bone scoffed. "Just listen to yourself. He loved himself, end of. You know he mocked you when you visited him in prison. He called *you* his vessel."

"I will end you," Tennyson growled. "As he has commanded."

"So why are you bothering with my ex? She's got nothing to do with this. Meiklejohn wouldn't waste his breath on her."

"We want you to suffer the way we have suffered."

"Why don't you let her go, then you can concentrate all your efforts on blowing me to pieces."

"It's a BOGOF deal." Her cackle bounced off the walls.

"He visits me, you know. I bet he doesn't visit you."

"You're a fucking liar!"

"Oh yes, most nights. He warned me about you. I think he wanted me to stop you."

"Shut your face."

"I honestly believe he wants me to forgive him. It's his atonement," Bone persisted.

"His atonement will be your death," Tennyson retorted.

"Just give it up, Tennyson. There are more guns out there than a Mafia wedding." He nodded to the battery of police lights glaring through the front window. "You've served in the army. You should know more than anyone when to cut your losses and surrender."

"Not before you die!" she cried out and raised her fist, but before she could press the button, the rear door flew open.

Alice rushed in and struck Tennyson on the side of the head with a shovel, knocking her sideways on to the floor and sending the detonator flying. Bone jerked back in surprise as the shovel narrowly missed his head.

Alice stood still for a second, panting as blood cascaded down her face from a deep wound on her forehead.

Down but not quite out, Tennyson slithered towards the detonator lying by the window.

Regaining her strength, Alice tore over to the woman and struck her again on the back of the head. Tennyson crumpled into a bloody heap, groaning.

Alice quickly ran to Bone and untied his wrists, then stood back in alarm when she saw the vest. "What do I do?" She wrung her hands in terror.

"Where's the detonator?" Bone asked.

"I think it's over there." Alice turned but stopped still when she saw Tennyson standing by the window, clutching the switch.

"Don't you dare!" Alice said and picked up the shovel.

"Oh no." Tennyson lifted her arm "I'm coming, my darling," she cried out, and her thumb moved above the switch.

Then, suddenly, Mullens burst through the door, flanked by two armed officers.

"Hey, Little Miss Sunshine!" he hollered. Raising a taser, he fired, and the barbed cable shot out of the gun and embedded in Tennyson's neck.

The electrical charge crackled, her face contorted, and she dropped like a sack of battered turnips to the floor. The two officers raced over and grappled with her convulsing arms and legs.

"About time," Bone called over. "Cuff her."

"What the fuck is that?" Mullens recoiled at the sight of the tangle of wires around Bone's chest.

"The straps," Bone pulled gently at the Velcro ties on the side of the vest.

"Shouldn't the response unit deal with this?" Mullens glanced over his shoulder at the ARVs.

"No time. She might have pressed the button — we don't know how long we have. Do it."

"Oh Christ." Mullens teased one of the straps. He stopped and considered the vest. "Maybe…"

"Wait — what are you doing?" Bone said. "No! That's an order!"

"Fuck this," Mullens exclaimed, and with brute force, he yanked the vest from Bone's chest. Gathering it up like a newborn baby, he careered out into the compound, hollering, "Police! Police! Don't shoot me, ya bampots!"

Alice sat on the floor and then rolled onto her side.

"Alice!" Bone said, and staggered over to her. "Medical assistance!" he hollered, and then hollered again.

Moments later, two anxious paramedics appeared at the door, followed by a flank of armed officers. One of the medics attended to Tennyson, while the second checked Alice.

"That's quite a gash," the medic said to Bone as she knelt.

Bone reached up and touched his bleeding face. "I've had worse. Is she all right?"

The medic checked the wound on Alice's head, and Alice let out a quiet moan.

"She just blacked out. She'll have a very sore head, but hopefully nothing too serious," the medic tried to reassure Bone.

Alice opened her eyes, and then a moment later, slowly sat up, clutching her head.

"Steady there." The paramedic took hold of her arm.

Alice mumbled incoherently, her eyes glazed.

"She's concussed," the paramedic said. "We'll get her to the ambulance."

Bone helped them shift Alice onto a stretcher, and they headed to the door.

"DCI Bone. Coming out." He stepped into a battery of blinding lights and a line of armed cops with their weapons primed on him.

The line parted, and the paramedics carried Alice through to the ambulance parked up at the entrance.

"Mark!" Bone scanned the wall of faces, but he couldn't see him. "Where did Detective Mullens go?" he shouted at one of the armed officers.

A loud explosion boomed out across the farmyard.

"Jesus!" Bone cried. He turned to run round the side of the office building, but the armed officer grabbed him.

"Not so fast, Inspector," the man insisted.

"He's one of my men," Bone hollered and attempted to shake off his grip.

"Is that them?" the ARP said with a grin.

Mullens and the two PCs from the car chase appeared, shuffling slowly towards the line. They were smothered from head to toe in some kind of muddy substance. The smell arrived before they even reached the line.

"What the hell, Mark?" Bone asked.

"I threw the bloody thing in the slurry pit. Thought that was the safest place. He wiped a thick layer of liquidised cow shit from his eyes and mouth.

"Looks like you've made a couple of new pals." Bone nodded towards the two car chase PCs who were busy shaking the glutinous poo from their hair.

A Mexican wave of laughter rolled along the police line.

FORTY

The Matron glanced up from her files and pointed up the ward. "Right at the end on the left-hand side."

Bone nodded and continued in. When Michael saw his mum, he dropped Bone's hand, ran to her bed, and leapt into her arms.

"Aw, my wee boy." Alice hugged him for dear life.

"Careful, Michael. Your mum's hurt her head, like you did the other day."

Alice kissed her son's forehead and cheeks. Michael pulled away and touched the strip of white plaster clinging to her forehead.

"Are you okay, Mummy?"

"I'm fine. I just fell off the climbing frame."

"Did Barry Hutchison push you off?"

"He did and he's a right one," she said with a giggle, gently tickling her son.

He wriggled free and dropped off the bed.

"Are you really okay?" Bone asked.

"Yes." Alice nodded reassuringly. "Just a bit of concussion, apparently. I should be getting home later today."

Glancing round the ward, Bone spotted a few toys stacked up by the window. "Hey, Michael, check those out." He pointed at a couple of plastic trucks. "Shall we go and have a look?"

"Yeah!" Michael yelled enthusiastically.

"Shh!" Alice said, holding her finger to her lips.

Bone took Michael over to the play area, and when the boy had settled in, Bone returned to Alice.

"Is Mum okay?" she asked.

"She's fine. Tough as a steel toecap, your mum. Anyway, I made sure they were both safe in the house." He sat on the edge of the bed. "Thank you."

"What for?"

"Well, aside from everything, lumping that lunatic with a shovel. That was quite a move."

"I didn't know I had it in me, to be honest. All I could think about was Michael."

"I'm so sorry for putting you all in danger. I fucked up."

"That woman did that, not you." Alice watched her son dismantle one of the trucks and stack the dismembered parts in the trailer of the second. She turned back to Bone. "You know when I said you could babysit?"

"Yes, and I managed to screw that up as well."

"I meant it. I want you to see more of your son. It's not fair, and I should have been kinder to you about that."

"Really, even after all this?"

"I know that you will do anything to keep Michael safe."

"And you," Bone said.

He reached for her hand, but she gently shifted it away.

"We can't go back. The two of us."

"I thought you maybe wanted to have another go."

"No. I'm sorry, Duncan."

Bone studied her face, and he could see her pain transforming into relief. He nodded. "I know. You're right. You always are."

"And always will be." She smiled. "But Michael belongs to both of us and was born out of love. And we need to cherish that."

Michael appeared, clutching a truck in one hand and a set of wheels in the other. "Can you fix it, Dad?" He thrust the broken vehicle into Bone's hands.

"Yeah, sure," Bone said with a bleary-eyed smile.

EPILOGUE

The sun had come out for the day and blessed Kilwinnoch Town Gardens with radiant blue sky. Despite Bone's appeal to keep the ceremony a quiet, informal affair, most of the staff from the three stations had turned up, along with a couple of bigwigs from Edinburgh, including the chief constable, Peter Laverty. Relatives, friends, members of community groups, and well-wishers were all gathered round the granite plinth set in the heart of a bed of brightly-coloured plants and flowers.

"Morning, sir." Walker sidled up next to Bone. "Sun's out," she added.

Bone glanced over to Mullens who was flanked by his wife and DS Baxter, immaculately dressed in a tweed trouser suit and scarf fit for a John Buchan novel. To her right was Will Harper, leaning on a set of crutches. He looked up, spotted Bone, and nodded back to him. Gallacher stepped forward.

"Thank you all for coming today." He cleared his throat. "We are here to honour the memory of our wonderful and well-loved colleagues. It is such a heart-warming sight to see so many people here today. Our community owes a huge debt to the sacrifice our police officers made to protect us all from harm. Each and every one of these courageous young women and men reached way above and beyond their duty." He then slowly read out every victim's name, pausing after each one. "They are heroes in the purest sense of the word," he continued. "Heroes of the police force, heroes of our town, and heroes of our nation, and we give thanks to them in every possible way." He turned to the plinth and a gleaming brass plate with all the names engraved in a neat column. "So let this plaque stand as a memory to our heroes and serve as a permanent reminder of their lives, their sacrifice, and their love for us all."

He bowed his head and wiped a tear from his eye.

The Rev. McIntyre stepped forward and for once delivered a succinct and poignant prayer. Right on cue, the Town Centre Parish church bells rang out across the town and the hills beyond. Someone from the back of the congregation clapped, and it quickly spread through the crowd, their collective applause joining the bells in a deafening crescendo of defiance and unity.

After a brief conversation with Gallacher and the vicar, and a quick check to see how Harper was holding up, Bone returned to his car. Walker caught up with him.

"That was emotional," Walker said, catching him before he ducked away.

"I'd rather they were all still alive," Bone replied.

"Yes, but they will be remembered forever, and for families, that helps keep them alive in their hearts."

"DS Mullens scrubbed up well for the occasion," Bone said with a smile.

Walker giggled. "So where did you get the money for the plinth?"

"Who told you that?" Bone said in surprise.

"A little bird, well, DS Baxter to be honest."

"Ach, I was hoping to keep that quiet."

"So?"

"You know that Davis album I showed you?"

"The signed one that belonged to your dad?"

"Auctioned it."

"I thought it was a cherished heirloom?"

"Nah, I've always hated Miles Davis — so overrated." Bone grinned. "Anyway, the force made up the difference," he lied.

They carried on to Bone's newly returned, washed, and valeted Saab, gleaming like a bright-green tree frog in the sunshine.

"Do you need a lift?"

"Every fibre of my being is screaming at me to say no, but it's actually quite good to see it back where it should be." She smiled.

"So am I the only person on the planet who can't decipher Morse code?" Bone asked.

"Turns out that Will studied it at uni."

"Now why does that not surprise me?"

Opening the passenger door, she lifted an envelope resting on the passenger seat and climbed in. She glanced at McKinnon's name and *The Chronicle* address on the front.

"Love letter?" she asked.

"Of sorts." Bone turned the starter on the Saab. It coughed, spluttered, coughed again, and then whimpered into life. "Let's just say, some information from an anonymous source is about to make Chief Officer McLean's life very interesting indeed."

"And all innocent parties protected, I hope?" Walker added.

"Oh, it's not from me." Bone smiled. "I'm just posting it for a favour."

He crunched the gear stick into first, and the car slowly rolled out of the car park.

The End

DCI BONE IS BACK IN...

Blood Water Falls

A DCI Bone Scottish Crime Thriller (Book 2)

You can't drown the dead

When the brutally murdered body of a local geography teacher is discovered at Kilwinnoch's famous beauty spot, Blood Water Falls, the community is rocked to its core.

For DCI Duncan Bone, the killing appears to be an open and shut case. But it's not long before a sinister clue unleashes dark and deadly forces, blowing the investigation wide open, and putting Bone and his team in grave danger.

With the town baying for blood, and too many suspects and not enough answers, DCI Bone faces not only the toughest case of his career, but the battle of his life to defeat the psychological demons determined to destroy him once and for all.

Set among the dramatic hills and glens of Scotland's Campsie Fells, *Blood Water Falls* is the second in a series of edge-of-your-seat crime thrillers that will keep you guessing right up to the nail-biting, heart-stopping climax.

Perfect for fans of Ian Rankin, J.D. Kirk, Val McDermid and Stuart MacBride.

Buy now on Amazon

Also on Kindle Unlimited

JOIN MY DCI BONE VIP CLUB

AND RECEIVE YOUR *FREE* DCI BONE NOVEL

WHAT HIDES BENEATH

Secrets Always Surface

Scotland's hottest summer on record is already too much for DCI Duncan Bone. As if the water shortage wasn't enough, a body turning up at the bottom of Kilwinnoch's dried up reservoir sends Bone to boiling point.
With three suspects on the loose and time running out, the Rural Crime Unit needs to find the smoking gun and nail the killer before another victim is slain.

Visit tgreid.com to sign up and download for *FREE*.

Your monthly newsletter also includes updates, exclusives, sneak peeks, giveaways and more…

THE DCI BONE SCOTTISH CRIME SERIES

Dark is the Grave

Blood Water Falls

Dead Man's Stone

The Killing Parade

Isle of the Dead

Night Comes Falling

Burn it all Down

More thrillers by TG Reid

Agency 'O'

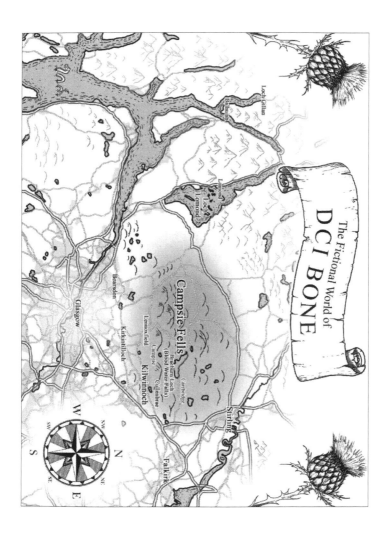

The Fictional World of
DCI BONE

ACKNOWLEDGEMENTS

I am forever indebted to the tireless help, support, expert advice, and encouragement I received from the following people. I owe you big time.

Emmy Ellis
Diana Hopkins
Meg Jolly
Kath Middleton
Gordon Robertson
Beverly Sandford
Steve Worsley (the voice of DCI Bone)
Lisa Wright
My wonderful Arc Team - Go the Boners!
UKCBC and CWA Facebook Crime Clubs
And

Jeni and Erin x

Printed in Great Britain
by Amazon